JACOB'S ART

Jacob's Art

Merryn Fergusson

A Novel

First published in Great Britain in 2021 by Sea Pink.

Copyright © Merryn Fergusson 2021

Merryn Fergusson has asserted her right under the Copyright, Designs and Patents Act 1988 to be identified as the author of this work.

Every reasonable effort has been made to trace copyright holders of material reproduced in this book, but if any have been inadvertently overlooked the publishers would be glad to hear from them.

Edited, designed and produced by Tandem Publishing
http://tandempublishing.yolasite.com/

The front cover image was painted by the artist Henry Israel, reproduced by kind permission of his daughter Becky Tabram.

ISBN: 978-1-5272-9786-9

10 9 8 7 6 5 4 3 2 1

A CIP catalogue record for this book is available from the British Library.

Printed and bound in Great Britain by CPI Group (UK) Ltd, Croydon CR0 4YY.

To Iain, Dougal and Chris

The character of Jacob is drawn from my acquaintance with, and admiration for, Henry Israel (1933–2017). All other characters are fictional.

PROLOGUE

Reuben stood in front of the noticeboard that hung on the centre wall of the entrance to the senior school. Announcements of all main events, prize winners, sporting successes, or exam results were pinned on the green baize surface. Every day a new piece of paper was affixed, replacing the out of date with unseemly haste. With four drawing pins he fixed the poster in a prominent position. This recent poster was the most colourful because it featured a brilliant band of yellow flanked by azure and marine. It was the flyer for his father's exhibition.

There was no mistaking the scene portrayed in bold oil paints. A bulge of headland richly crowned with corn above an extensive stretch of bay was surrounded by an infinite sea and a summer-blue sky. The artist did not need to sully raw nature with details; no gulls flew, no windbreaks interrupted the expanse of sand, no people or tractors dotted the landscape. There was no indication that time had passed since Creation.

With suppressed pride Reuben remained fixed and hoped that his unmoving figure would attract the attention of his classmates to the noticeboard. It was not necessary. Reuben's family name was unique in the school and everybody knew about his father's exhibition, but he could not resist provoking a reaction. If he heard some expression of admiration or incredulity, it might reassure him that the event advertised on the flyer was real; an acknowledgement that this was a pivotal moment.

What Reuben wanted, more than any comment, however, was for everything to change. He was not dissatisfied with his life, in fact, he considered that he was well-adjusted and able to cope with his family's unusual method of earning a living, one that meant, despite his father giving evening classes, that money was tight, but he was aware that it had its shortcomings. Reuben's strategy was to make a name for himself by not conforming to the preoccupation with fashion or modern gadgets. He had gained a certain prestige for his gutsy independent stance. However, he would like to see his parents able to afford a new car – jokes about it among his friends had ceased long ago – and he did wish there was a little more cash available for his sisters, as an incident that morning had illustrated.

"Where did you get that?"

It was Florrie's first term at the senior school and dangling keyrings from the zips of their school-bags was the current craze.

"What?" Florrie asked defiantly.

Reuben lifted up the koala bear keyring that Florrie had added to her collection.

Abigail, younger than Reuben but a year older than Florrie, hurried to make the peace. "She was probably given it."

"Were you?" Reuben persisted.

"I swapped it."

"What for?"

Florrie mumbled an answer.

"What for, Florrie?"

"Some of my dinner money."

"You paid for it? Why would you spend money on a bear? What did you do for dinner?"

"I made a sandwich, if you want to know. I made it and hid it. Why can't I buy a koala if I want one? All the other girls have loads of mascots."

"Leave it!" begged Abigail. "They all have them in her year. You can't be different, not in first year. It's all right for you."

"Why is it all right for me?"

"You've made your friends."

Reuben faced his sister. "And you think they'll be her friends now? We don't have money to burn, you know."

"It's a keyring, Reuben, have a sense of proportion. Don't take everything so seriously, that's life when you are an artist. You should know that."

He felt annoyed with himself for being upset with Florrie. He did understand her predicament, but, as he and Abigail had learnt, she would have to decide which matters were important. Bears on keyrings did not create more or better friendships than being without bears on keyrings.

He had more sympathy with Abigail. While her friends were dyeing their hair, experimenting with makeup or inviting her on shopping trips, Abigail stoutly declared that she was not interested and that because she was going to be a painter like their father she had to learn to be frugal. Her use of this word had impressed her friends quite as much as her resolve.

Yet now, this exhibition, the culmination of years of work, was set to propel his father towards a deserved recognition.

"Who'll come to your Dad's exhibition?" A girl joined Reuben beside the noticeboard.

"Art critics and buyers."

"And some time wasters would come for the free drinks?"

She had not meant to sound hurtful but Reuben answered

abruptly. "Not at a proper exhibition like this one."

"Oh!" She adjusted rapidly. "It's at the Tower Gallery, that's quite something."

"My Dad says he's going," another girl chipped in.

"Thanks," Reuben replied.

At that moment his classmates arrived and he was surrounded.

"Wow! I wish my Dad would do something like that!"

"Will he sell them for loads of money?"

"Of course he will, paintings sell for hundreds of pounds." The boys' comments followed each other without Reuben having to reply. He drifted into the classroom in the midst of his friends, buoyed by their enthusiasm and confidence.

At the end of the week the flyer had gone, replaced by a notice for the Christmas Fair, and Reuben walked by without an upward glance. In his school-bag were the reviews, cut from various newspapers, in which Reuben hoped to find just one that endorsed his conviction that his father was a talented artist. Each journalist described their incomprehension of his father's style and composition and wondered how their well-known landscape could become so unrecognisable.

Reuben avoided his friends and they reciprocated. How could he face them when only three paintings had been sold, and those to loyal acquaintances. He felt the rejection more strongly even than his father, who accepted the outcome philosophically; they had covered their costs.

Unlike his father, Reuben could not hide in an artist's studio. He had to face his school friends with his father's failure on his shoulders. He vowed that he would work towards a career that gave his family financial security, and that in future he would do everything in his power to prevent his father from suffering another public humiliation.

"I heard about the exhibition." The girl from the previous week walked alongside him.

Reuben had nothing to say.

"At least he sold some paintings, sometimes no paintings at all get sold."

"Thanks."

"It's just bad luck. That's all."

ONE

Reuben pushed open the door. It was never locked, but in his eagerness to be back with his family he did not notice Tansy's look of surprise.

Matty was waiting for him. "Reuben. You're here." He bent down to give his youngest sister a hug. She looked over his shoulder, curious to see the girl who Reuben wanted to introduce to them. "Hello, Tansy," she said formally.

Tansy did not know what to expect but Matty's greeting was disconcerting and she wondered if she was a disappointment. The kitchen filled with Reuben's family. His mother greeted her, and then his sisters, Abigail and Florrie. His father, Jacob, was the last to enter. He was dressed in a worn thick cotton shirt, battered leather waistcoat where lost buttons were mismatched with torn buttonholes, and baggy cord trousers that had seen many a hard-working day.

"Welcome, Tansy. It's always chaotic here." He said this with pride rather than apology, indicating the room. Every surface was cluttered with books, papers, art materials and pottery and paintings hung in every space on the walls. "So you survived the journey? Those lanes can make a person feel squeamish."

"I'm a good traveller if I'm driving. I was more worried for Reuben."

"He's used to those roads, and it's a luxury for him to be driven. The bus takes for ever. Come, we're about to eat."

"You're sitting by me," Matty said, pulling out a chair at the large wooden table. Tansy was grateful because Reuben was talking to his father and forgetting that she might need to take her cue from him. In one respect his assumption that his sisters would look after her, or that she could look after herself, was reassuring.

"What's for dinner Deborah?" Jacob asked.

"Beef casserole." His wife placed a large dish in the centre of the table.

Tansy could sense Matty sizing her up. "I do like your boots," Matty said quietly.

"They're wonderfully warm," Tansy answered, "it's cold in Glasgow."

"It's cold in this house too, but it's worse for you."

"Why's that?"

"Reuben said that you lived in Africa. It's hot there isn't it?"

"Sometimes too hot! But we went to cooler places too, in the hills or on the beach." It sounded too exotic. "Your house is cosy. A real home."

Tansy smiled at Deborah. "This is delicious."

"Florrie helped me. Jacob grows most of the vegetables. We are reasonably self-sufficient."

"What Mother means is that we don't go to the super-market," Abigail explained.

"Oh! I have to."

"Of course you do, you live in a city," Deborah said kindly.

"Are those Jacob's paintings on the walls?" Tansy asked. Predominantly country scenes and flowers, they were painted with a light touch of the brush and with a gentle selection of colours.

"Those are Mother's, she did them at college," Matty answered. "She says that she hasn't had any time since we came along." She emphasised the last few words as if they were a family mantra. "But she's no excuse now that I am at the academy."

Deborah, her wispy hair partially covering her forehead, arranged the saucepans on the range and then turned to reply.

"One day," she and Matty said in unison.

"Dad's are in the mill, they are too big for the house."

Jacob looked up when he heard his name and broke off his conversation with Reuben. Tansy caught Reuben's eye. She thought that he approved.

"Do you all paint?" Tansy made an effort to include Florrie and Abigail. Florrie's head was down, avoiding the question.

Abigail tipped her head towards Florrie. "Some of us more than others." She then fixed her eye on Jacob but he seemed in no hurry to speak.

Finally he said, "Abigail wants to go to art school."

"My future is not up for discussion," Abigail said, addressing her father. "It's not fair. It's not a subject for a family debate, especially since Tansy's here."

Tansy wondered if Abigail resented her visit, or whether she was trying to spare her from witnessing an argument.

"Tansy doesn't want to hear us going over this again."

"We don't know Tansy's views on art college," Jacob ignored Abigail and smiled congenially, "do we?"

Deborah pre-empted her. "Well, you know my views on that one!" She looked across to her husband with a knowing grin.

"Deborah was at art school herself but would not advise it for anyone else."

"So how would you learn?"

No one around the table hurried to answer Tansy's question. She glanced at Deborah who seemed pleased that she had spoken up. She answered Tansy with a soft smile. "How do you learn to be an artist? How did artists learn before there were institutions? They worked at their craft in attics, attended lessons in artists' studios and studied past masters."

Abigail went on the defensive. "Everyone goes to art college now. It's all very well saying that I should go and live in an attic and learn from other artists while washing up in a bar 'til the small hours, but times have changed and it's not like that anymore. You have to go to college. Artists' studios are places where the rich can go and dabble at painting, and they are probably all sexagenarians. Don't giggle, Matty. It's a perfectly respectable word.

"Sorry Dad!" she added apologetically, "I know that you have to give those classes."

"I chose to do that, Abi, and you are right!" Jacob assented.

"But how did they live, back in those days?" Tansy was curious.

Jacob leaned back in his chair. "They worked! There were no loans then to support student life. And no debts to hang over them! Don't tell me that an artist will ever earn enough to pay back a loan. I can't think why they were ever awarded. It's a downright scandal that hard-working taxpayers pay for no-hope artists."

"Wait for it Tansy, we're going to hear one of Dad's theories!" Abigail warned. "Is there an art faculty on your campus?"

Tansy appreciated her change of direction and rewarded her with a conspiratorial smile. "I wouldn't know!" she answered. "Until I met Reuben I didn't know a Monet from a Manet and I gave up drawing when I was in primary."

Tansy noticed that many of the paintings that were hung

on the walls around the kitchen were unframed. The two small windows had sun-bleached curtains, the loose covers and the carpet were threadbare, and every item of furniture was worn. This was the reality of living with an artist who eschewed the commercial outlets and refused all offers of salaried employment in an educational institution.

Tansy was beginning to understand why Reuben chose the subject that he was studying. "So, that explains the business studies?"

Reuben nodded and then said, "It's all very well, Abi, going to art school if you know what you want to do and why you are doing it, but if you don't they'll mess with your head. There are a whole lot of phoneys out there speaking the lingo but without a clue why they are there. In many cases it's seen as an easy option to delay any serious decision. That's my objection to it. How can you know at eighteen what you want to do for the rest of your life? Speaking for myself, I hadn't an idea. I still don't. Most occupations require an understanding of business. You wouldn't go far wrong in doing that course first, Abi."

Tansy persisted. "Deborah, you and Jacob went to art school?" Deborah looked across at her husband.

Jacob answered with a grin. "We did! And look where it took us! Away from the city to this remote place and existing on the fruit of our labours and the odd evening class, inflicting our convictions on the next generation!"

Reuben's sisters, Abigail, Florrie and Matty, were unsophisticated and their dress unfashionable. "That might change?" Tansy suggested, indicating Reuben.

Jacob laughed. "He takes after his grandfather. A secure and steady income, and an incomprehension of the simple life." He would not let Reuben interrupt. "It's all right, Reuben. I understand your decision. No need for you to adopt this life just because it suits your mother and me."

"But you are artists," Tansy argued, "you can live here, not everyone can. In any case, artists need to learn and it seems to me that they would need to go to college."

Until this moment Matty and Florrie had been content to listen to the adults but as Matty set her knife and fork beside each other on her empty plate she took the opportunity of the pause in conversation to announce, "Well, I'm going to art college."

Jacob was amused. "And when did you decide this?"

"When we learnt that there are hardly any women artists. All the artists in your books are men."

"Not exactly," Jacob began.

"There's Jessie King," said Florrie, supporting her father. "We did a project on her."

"Because she lived and worked near here. I mean there were no famous women in the olden days."

Jacob gave a gentle nod of his head. "You have a point there, Matty."

Florrie continued. "And there's Mother."

"I mean really famous. I'm going to be a famous painter," Matty insisted.

"Then you had better start saving. You'll never have any money and always be poor," Florrie said with a flourish and stood up to indicate that she had won her point and that everyone could hand her their plates.

"Give her a hand, Matty," Deborah prompted.

"So on balance, what do you think, Tansy?" Jacob asked.

"It seems a precarious way to earn a living." Tansy registered that this might be a judgement on Jacob's way of life and so hurried on. "I mean, you have to be totally dedicated. Not many artists make a fortune, like Vettriano."

Almost every café in Glasgow hung a Vettriano on their walls and only the unobservant could fail to notice his work. It did not take a connoisseur to know his name or be aware of his rise to fame. It was also common knowledge that his commercial success caused irritation to self-styled real artists.

"You have to be dead before a painting has any value," Reuben said. "The longer you are dead the more valuable your work becomes. The public should support artists."

"Why should they?" Jacob challenged. "No one asked me to paint. I chose it. We've managed and I would not have had it differently. Just because I can't live without my painting, it doesn't mean that other people need it."

"Surely there was a need in everyone, somewhere, for beautiful or thought-provoking objects outside the purely utilitarian." Tansy wondered if Reuben was unconsciously quoting his father and was surprised to see him so animated. "There should be some way that this could change. So that dead artists don't get all the money."

"It's not the dead artists," corrected Deborah, "it's the dealers."

"And they make millions while a real artist, who will one day be a future Da Vinci or Van Dyke, starves," Reuben said dramatically. He looked around the table and then he smiled at Abigail to show that he was in sympathy with her even if he appeared to be arguing against her bid to go to college.

Florrie and Matty each carried a bowl from the scullery. "The cream is in the fridge," Deborah reminded them.

"I hope you're not pursuing a career in the arts," Jacob asked Tansy with a twinkle. Tansy saw three faces turn towards her.

"I'm studying creative writing. I met Reuben because our departments share the same common room."

"I have always wondered," Jacob said thoughtfully as the dessert was passed round, "what would happen if there was a way that every time a painting changed hands the artist received a commission, a percentage, a royalty, perhaps only for the duration of their lifetime." He seemed to be speaking to himself. "Paintings have become a vehicle for transferring money. Beyond their intrinsic artistic value, once a painting has a reputation its value continues to increase. Is there a way of directing money to living artists, so that an artist could profit from the sale of their painting each time that it changed hands? Or, perhaps, after a while a painting could become valueless, like books, which lose their copyright after a set number of years." He chuckled quietly, not caring if anyone was listening. "Just think of the consequences!"

Tansy noticed that Deborah was alert to his thoughts. "Enabling money to be targeted to existing artists?" It was as if she had not heard Jacob on this train of thought before.

Tansy picked up on the chemistry between them. "That would be revolutionary," she commented.

TWO

Tansy woke early and, because they had arrived in the dark, felt disorientated. Without disturbing Abigail whose room she shared, she pulled on her clothes and quietly made her way down the stairs. The kitchen was warm from the range but the sudden chill of the scullery made her reach for a coat. There was an array of jackets and leggings on the hooks by the door, all of them well-worn, and she chose one that she assumed was Deborah's. It had a fur lining to the hood and it fitted adequately, the belt fastened even if the zip appeared to be broken.

The door caught against the stone tiles once it was part-way opened, but being slight, Tansy slipped through the gap to the outside, not wanting to tug at the handle and create a noise. She closed the door to keep the cold from entering the house, and hugging her coat around her, stepped away. It was only partially light but the dew glistened on the path which led around the house. On all sides stunted trees, their height halted by the constant winds which blew from the nearby coast, sheltered the building. Smoke trailed from one chimney but it felt to Tansy as if the house, like its occupants, was sleeping. In the windows the curtains were drawn, like closed eyelids. There was no birdsong apart from, high above her, the odd squawking of a gull, no sound of vehicles, no voices. She could see no lights and the air smelt of damp grass. Tansy could not recall ever experiencing such isolation.

She followed the path, slabs laid at random edged by grass on one side and a narrow earth border against the house on the other, around to the front of the house. This was where they had entered the previous night, when a light glowed above the door and from behind the curtains of the windows on either side. Now she could see the whitewashed walls, dulled from age and mud-spattered at the base from the flowerless borders. She noticed tufts of grass growing from the gutters, and remains of nests under the eaves. Spiders' webs filled the angles of the window frames and leaves collected on the sills. Something to do with its timelessness and its association with Reuben gave it a touch of romance. Without him it would have been unremarkable, just another farmhouse, but because this one had been singled out, enabling her to become familiar with it, the house was already gaining a personality. The house, the garden and the wall that marked out the extent of their ground, created a world apart. No one in a city was separated from others to this extent. Tansy wondered if this led to a more individual approach to life and whether it was this spirit of independence that had attracted her to Reuben.

She had long recognised that in Nigeria she had been brought up with different opinions to those she encountered among the majority of the students with whom she studied, but she enjoyed the novelty. However, she understood how Reuben could also have developed an alternative approach to how adults could conduct their lives. Yet he had adopted the city. She expected that she would too.

At that moment she saw Matty, wearing a fluffy orange jacket over her pyjamas, and with her feet encased in a pair of oversized panda slippers, standing at the corner of the house. Tansy walked towards her. Matty's eyes were fixed on her, unsure.

"Matty! Is anyone else awake?"

Matty smiled, looked up at the windows above them and shook her head. "No, there's just you and me. Where are you going?"

"Nowhere particularly. Exploring."

Matty scanned the garden. "There's more to explore at the back. I'll show you if you like."

Tansy could hear the eagerness in her voice but pointing to Matty's feet she answered, "Later?"

She was rewarded with a shy grin and followed Matty back along the path. As they hung up their coats Matty asked, "After breakfast?" Then she hesitated. "If Reuben doesn't mind."

However, Reuben had other plans. "We're going into town. What is it, Matty?" he asked when he saw her scowl. "You can come too, and Florrie. Don't you want to show Tansy around?"

Tansy caught Matty's eye. "Later?"

"You seem to know everyone in the town," Tansy commented, once they had finished the circuit of the main street and the harbour, and called at one or two shops for purchases for Deborah.

"It may appear so and I suppose we do know most, but not very well," Matty answered. "Reuben says that I am quite a little gossip," she mimicked his way of speaking, "but he's no better. We recognise a lot of people because we go to school there."

"It is a very small community."

"Compared to Glasgow, certainly."

When they returned to the house Matty insisted on taking Tansy on a tour of the garden, and then, through a gate in the wall, towards the nearby hill. "You can see for miles from up there."

They walked along the outside of the field where it was bounded by a burn. Although the grass was well cropped by the sheep beside the banks, under the trees the grass grew thickly in tufts. The branches hung low over the edge of the burn, impeding their progress along a path that had been worn by the regular passage of feet.

They stood for a while in a gap between the trees and watched the water as it whirled in eddies around large boulders or rushed through gullies as it converged to funnel between adjacent rocks. Debris, broken twigs and dead leaves collected where the water lay in pools. The water glinted in the weak sunlight and gurgled and splashed as it poured relentlessly past them.

Tansy reached up to a branch above her, fingered a leaf bud and then held one of the long yellow tendrils that hung together in a bunch.

"That's a catkin. When we were small we called them lambs' tails." Matty told her. "The tree is a hazel." She moved ahead of Tansy, searching until she pointed to a darker set of hanging tails. "These are alder. They have tiny black cones as well."

They climbed away from the burn and clambered up the hill, Matty leading the way. At the top, boulders formed a rocky outcrop. Choosing a flattened surface she sat down calling to Tansy, "Come and see!"

In the distance they could see the estuary and, where it joined the sea, islands, bays and inlets. Below them the hillside was dotted with grazing sheep.

"You are so lucky, you know, Tansy."

Tansy, who had the same thought about her companion, saw Matty's worried frown. "And you're not?"

Surprised, Matty glanced briefly towards Tansy and then fixed her gaze on the landscape.

"I don't think so. You see, you have been brought up abroad and must know so much about the world. Where did you go to school? Are there schools in Nigeria, I mean, where you can do exams like we do? You must have had to do exams to go to university."

"I did British exams at my boarding school. It was weekly boarding."

"And you travelled and know how people live in other countries."

Tansy smiled. "But I didn't know how people lived in this country. And now you are helping me learn that."

"Really?" Matty beamed, stretched and faced Tansy. "Really?"

"This morning, when we went to the butcher's, you knew which farm he was describing when he said where the beef came from."

"Yes?" Matty was puzzled.

"Well, I had never thought like that. I don't look at a field of sheep and then link it up with lamb chops on his counter."

Matty screwed up her face. "Everyone knows that."

From where they were sitting they could see acres of hillside in every direction. Behind them the hills grew in height in soft undulations, marked out by stone dykes and interrupted by blocks of planted firs. On the horizon there was evidence of extensive forestry. The coast stretched on either side, the pebble beach leading down to the sea.

"When the tide is out you can walk across to that island where they take the sheep to graze in the summer.

Over there is the Isle of Man and those hills are in the Lakes." Matty pointed out the landmarks, but Tansy was unfamiliar with the place names and instead saw it as a canvas that a painter might want to capture. Artists would be drawn to this area, this she could understand.

"Can I ask you something, Tansy?" Matty's face was puckered and she tucked her hands into her sleeves. "I feel different, at school. My Dad doesn't go to work, we don't go on holidays, or go shopping for clothes at the weekend, like everyone else."

"You feel like an outsider?"

Matty nodded. "Do you feel like that?"

"I did, when I first arrived, but then I realised that everyone is an outsider, and everyone feels like that."

"Even Louisa? She's the leader of the set of girls everyone wants to be friends with."

"Probably Louisa more than most. She thinks that if she is surrounded by other girls she'll be part of something that she thinks exists. She thinks that she will be the same as everyone else."

"But she's not?"

Looking across the vast sweep of the coast it was easy to see how those living on farms and in remote cottages must feel isolated, but were they more isolated from others than city dwellers, where people in adjacent flats of terraced houses might not know their neighbours?

"We are all outsiders in our own way. Each of us unique."

They started back down the hill and the path soon led between high gorse bushes. Matty stopped to pick a spindly stem from below the hedgerow. She waited until the path widened and then showed Tansy. "This is shepherd's purse," she said as they walked beside each other. "But Tansy, that's not useful stuff."

"You don't think so? Tell me the name of your favourite wild flower."

"Ragged Robin."

"Describe it."

"It's pink, about this high, you see it in summer and every petal is split and, well, ragged."

"It sounds beautiful, Matty, but it took a lot of describing. If you spoke to a botanist they would know immediately what you were referring to."

"Knowing about Ragged Robin isn't any use. Not in the real world."

"You don't know that. You could say that about anything, but you have to build up knowledge and you have to start somewhere. Whether its maths, grammar, nature. You see, you need a common language if you want to communicate."

The impact of the land penetrated every moment of the day except when at school. Matty was in tune with the seasons and her surroundings in a way that was not possible in a city.

"Give me the name of a painter," Tansy said.

"Monet."

"I've heard of him, lilies and landscapes."

"He's an Impressionist."

"Now that I know this we have a common language, and that makes us less different."

"So everything is important?"

"You never know when you will use it, but knowledge helps us to build links between people. The more we learn the more people we can connect with."

They reached the field and climbed over the gate, retracing their steps.

"Tansy," Matty asked as she led the way along the path, "what are you going to do for a job?"

"I've been wondering about this for a long time, and I think that I have finally decided."

"Because of our conversation?" Matty sounded pleased.

"It has helped to crystallise my thinking. If I want to communicate with other people, I should be a journalist."

THREE

The university common room was large and uninspiring. There was one tired picture of the building, a vast Gothic edifice whose extravagant tower and multitude of small turrets dominated the surrounding landscape, but no other wall hangings relieved the tired paintwork. The seats of the sofas and armchairs were so worn and thinly padded that, although they used them, the majority of the students found them uncomfortable. The floor was scuffed linoleum. The bar was a later addition and its overhead lights and mirrors reflecting off the chrome counter cheered up one end of the otherwise gloomy room. Reuben sat on one of the mock-leather-covered stools which were ranged along its length, but the paucity of students that day at the start of his final year only emphasised the drabness of the room. Reuben was about to leave when Tansy entered and, going directly to speak to the barman, appeared upset. She explained that she had lost her purse.

Everyone knew Tansy, if only from afar. She had made her mark in their freshers' week, as the glamorous girl who seemed to have the talent for every activity that was organised. Pretty and confident, she remained aloof from close relationships, friendly to all yet not singling out anyone. That had been the case for three years while Reuben watched her from a distance, but that day, everything changed.

Reuben never looked at Tansy without wondering what she had seen in him that she had not found in her previous relationships. Invariably Tansy, eye-catching in whatever she wore, was accompanied by sleek, good-looking men in buttoned-up shirts, fitted trousers, and well-cut jackets.

Uncomfortable in anything other than a t-shirt, baggy trousers with a myriad of pockets, and trainers, Reuben felt at a disadvantage. But, alone at the bar, Tansy exuded none of her usual confidence and sliding off his stool he walked towards her.

"Can I help?" he asked.

Surprised, Tansy turned, hardly registering him. "Yes. No. Perhaps." She seemed flustered. "My friends have left for the concert, but I've lost my purse. I said I would catch them later."

"That's not good. Losing your purse. You were sitting over there? Maybe it's fallen down beside one of the chairs." Tansy stood and watched as Reuben searched. "No. It's not here."

"No?" Tansy echoed and looked crestfallen.

"Can I lend you some money?" Reuben offered.

Tansy looked deflated and then sighed. Reuben, who had expected that she would want to chase after her friends, noticed her hesitation. He even wondered if she felt lonely. It seemed unlikely but the thought prompted him to ask, "Do you want a drink? To commiserate?" He feared that he had presumed too much. "You could still catch that concert."

"I don't know that I want to," Tansy stated, and then smiled. "I would like a drink."

Reuben pulled up a stool and sat beside her.

"My name's Tansy," she told him as she picked up her glass.

"I know."

"And yours is Reuben. Don't look surprised, you're not invisible!"

"I suppose not." Reuben shook his head and pushed the hair from his forehead. "You're in your last year too."

Tansy held her glass on her lap and her long fair hair partially covered her face. She seemed to be waiting for him to continue.

"What are your plans, for the summer?"

"I'll go back to my family. Is that what you will do?"

"I've had the same job every holiday. It's in the local pub. Where I live there are a lot of tourists and you take whatever job is going."

"That's good. I can't work in Nigeria, so I'm afraid I shall be a bit self-indulgent. Swimming and parties. It's different there."

"It's different where I come from, too." Reuben gave her a half-smile. "Not like that at all."

Reuben was relieved to see Tansy's face light up. "That's what I like about university! You come from I don't know where, and know everything about here, and I've had to learn it from scratch. Sometimes I put my foot in it."

"So do I."

Reuben's drink was finished and Tansy placed her empty glass on the counter.

"Can I walk you home?"

"I usually take the bus."

"I'll walk you to the stop. Let me pay your fare?"

"Just a loan?" He heard the hint of an invitation.

"That's a deal. Then I can see you again?"

Now, several months later and nearing the end of their last year, Tansy and a group of friends descended on the common room where the shortcomings of its furnishings and furniture became of little import. This group would soon disseminate, many of them beyond the bounds of the city, armed with a degree and in search of work. They settled haphazardly around a low table on which they deposited their bags. Tansy was bubbling with repressed excitement. She had news that she intended to save until Reuben arrived and to distract her she entered into the current topic of debate.

"I don't know much about the countryside, but you say that people who don't own their farm will have the right to buy it?" Tansy asked.

"Don't worry, you're not the only one who doesn't understand! If one group of society has a right to buy, why is this not rolled out across all commercial enterprises?" another chipped in.

"If it applies to farm tenants, why does it not apply to other people who rent, like hairdressers or butchers?"

"Or to tenants of flats, like us?" The laughter was unanimous.

"The principle is to try and help the disadvantaged and it is good, but it does not work in practice." Faces turned to the speaker who stated this as if the fact was obvious. "When they sold council houses to their owners, they bought them for a song, but after five years they were allowed to sell, the houses changed hands each time at a profit, and very soon those houses were unaffordable to other disadvantaged people."

Tansy persisted. "So now that rule might give the right to buy to tenants of farms?"

Another in the group objected. "It doesn't make sense in the long term. The tenant has the right to buy and that is advantageous for the tenant who becomes an owner. However, when that person, now an owner, becomes old, injured or wants to change direction, takes on a tenant, the cycle repeats itself. It solves nothing. It only benefits one generation. The same as council houses, the sales only benefitted the original incumbent."

Tansy's friends plied the original speaker, a girl who took every issue head on, with questions.

"So what's your point?"

Tansy tried another angle. "What if it applied to things that are not property? What about literature, music and art?"

"You can't compare them," the girl objected. "Music is accessible to everyone for a reasonable cost, whether sheet music or recorded. Anyone is able to play a Beethoven sonata. Books have a copyright and royalties are due for a limited time. In a way you are renting them, because no one owns them anymore. They become affordable for most people. That's why the classics are so cheap."

"It does not apply to artefacts; they can double or more in value, in time," Tansy interjected.

"What do you mean?"

"Art is quite different. Art can go on making money indefinitely, but the money does not go to the artist. Once there is a consensus that a work of art is valuable, each time it changes hands the price increases. Van Gogh died penniless but many years later his paintings were making millions for other people. The artist does not benefit but at each exchange the dealer makes a profit."

"You mean that there should be a law to stop dealers making so much money? How would that help the artist?"

Tansy took up the challenge as if she had already prepared her argument. "If there was a limit to the time that someone could own a painting or sculpture, or whatever, then the artefact would become valueless. I don't mean immediately, but perhaps there is a way in which the artist would get royalties and then it could be owned by everyone."

"No law could do that."

"You can't suddenly make something worthless."

"Why not? What about ivory?" Tansy countered. "Craftsmen made the most beautiful works of art from ivory, but now they are valueless. No one is allowed to sell them. But the real question is how to make things fairer when the solutions prove to have only limited success."

This sparked further discussion but Reuben was due to arrive and Tansy became restless. She glanced frequently towards the door and her concentration drifted. She wondered about Reuben's father, Jacob, and what drove him to reject an easier life, the sort that was reliant on a regular salary, for the vagaries of painting canvasses for an unreliable purchasing public. Was it possible that Reuben's father had no choice because the artistic gene was so dominant? There was something alluring about Jacob's reliance and dependence on nature for a living and his belief in his work, and Tansy was awed by his dedication. She was mystified by the concept of communicating through a medium that was wholly impractical and which relied totally on inspiration. She was intrigued by the artist's world, but she was glad that Reuben showed no signs of an artistic temperament and had chosen a career that could give him steady employment.

Her group of friends left the common room and Tansy remained behind. After a short while a sudden influx of students entered and Tansy felt a hand on her shoulder. "Reuben!" She spun round excitedly and, always reluctant to show affection in public, grasped his hand. He sat down close beside her. "Tell me, what is it?"

***

She recalled their first conversation, her unexpected reluctance to leave him to catch her bus, and the relief when he suggested that they should meet again. It had been the discovery of Reuben and his friends, where she could explore ideas without fear of ridicule, that had prompted Tansy to contemplate a career in journalism, recognising that it was a useful forum for debate. It was this aspect of their relationship, this freedom to discuss every topic, that had attracted her to Reuben initially.

Later, as she grew to trust him, she mentioned that she had the idea of attempting to become a journalist.

"Why not politics?" Reuben asked her. "Isn't that more in your line? Once you have an idea you want to see it come to fruition."

Tansy replied, "I want to help people, ordinary people."

"You can do that in either field," Reuben suggested.

"No, I can't. I am far too young to go into politics, and my ideas are probably infantile. I need experience. I have never had a full-time job, paid taxes, taken on a mortgage, so how can I make decisions that affect all the things regular people do?"

Reuben was not convinced. "Journalists are very persuasive. They too affect the way people think and act."

Tansy had her answer ready. "But at least people have a choice to accept or reject them!" she had told him.

Reuben considered this. "You have experience of the wider world which may be to your advantage when you try for a job. It's a tough world, I gather."

Reuben was unaware that his confidence in her, and his level-headed opinions gave him an enigmatic appeal. Tired of her superficial pleasures, Tansy was beginning to explore a deeper undercurrent in life and that evening had presented her with a gateway to a new relationship.

She asked Reuben about himself and as she listened to him she was astonished. "You would just go off for the day and wander among the hills or along the estuary and no one minded? Your parents knew and people did not think that it was odd? That is so exotic."

Reuben was amused. "My childhood appeared unremarkable. When we weren't helping Dad with the vegetables and if we could escape from the jobs Mum always had ready for us, we were free. We weren't as isolated as you imagine. People came for classes and we would talk to them. We were a bit precocious. We read all the time and discussed all the major artists and their works, so we were not really treated as children. Living in Nigeria, now that is exotic."

"In my childhood I was surrounded by adults. Contact was usually at barbecues and cocktail parties where I had to wear my best dress and hand round nuts and finger food. People did not notice me except to remark on my dress. They did not expect me to have opinions."

"I picture a small girl, lost in a crowded room where everyone's attention is fixed elsewhere. You are quite at ease now in company," Reuben observed, thinking of the last time that he had seen her, when she was the centre of an admiring crowd.

"I watched and I learnt, didn't I?" she teased. "But after a while it feels like a game where nothing is real."

"I am no good at that sort of game."

"It's not something that you need to be skilled at. I am beginning to realise that it is more difficult to resist conforming. The trouble is that I don't know who I am, whereas you do seem to know who you are."

"I do?"

Tansy made an exaggerated appraisal of his appearance.

"Oh that!" Reuben looked doubtful. "No one else had an eccentric artist as a father. Either I had to pretend to be someone else and try and fit in, or to brave it out."

"So you didn't mind?"

"I minded, but in the long run it was easier to be myself and hope I would be accepted. Eventually I did make some friends."

"I noticed."

"You did?"

"Of course I did. I thought that I would not be your type, but I wanted you to notice me."

Hesitantly, they both laughed and catching each other's eyes for the first time, they forged a link that had not been broken since.

From that moment Reuben and Tansy were inseparable.

***

Reuben now sat down, in a misshapen t-shirt and faded jeans, his hair a halo of uncontrolled curls, beside Tansy who seemed, even in her sleeveless top and cotton skirt, to dress with an effortless elegance. He leant forward to give her a kiss. "What is it you want to tell me?"

Tansy looked nervous. "Perhaps I am expecting too much. It might not happen. It's just…"

"No. It's something, it must be something," Reuben was persuasive. He placed a hand on hers and squeezed lightly.

"I might have a job," she said finally.

Work was a recurrent topic. Reuben had secured a job with a financial firm, and hoped that it would give him a foot on the ladder, but journalism was quite a different prospect. Reuben could not see how, by writing an article or two a week or even a column, Tansy could earn a living.

"Go on!"

"It's with *Inside and Out*. I've been writing some articles for them and they have asked me to apply for a new post that they have created."

Reuben's reaction was emphatic. "Not bad!" he said

slowly. *Inside and Out* was a relatively expensive glossy magazine that featured houses, patios and pocket-sized town gardens. It had been around for a few years and had become well established.

"I know it's a bit ironic, when this is how your family struggled, that I am trying to make a go of journalism with no fixed income. The magazine wants to attract a wider, more erudite, and hopefully more moneyed readership. It would be a column about current art exhibitions and artists."

"But you don't know anything about art!" Reuben was incredulous.

"That's the whole point! Who better to write it than someone who is not an artist."

"How will you know what to write?"

"Haven't I been listening to your father, and your mother, for that matter, not to mention you? What better training could I have had?"

Reuben laughed and gave a shrug of disbelief. "If anyone could succeed it would be you, Tansy! What have you got to do?"

"All applicants have to submit a thousand words. The only proviso is that it gains people's attention. They don't want 'a tutorial or a pictorial guide to the major artists over the last hundred years'," she quoted. "I don't need to know very much. That is why I think that I have a chance. They liked the article that I submitted on spec, and it's been published. I'll show you."

"Well, if you want a topic, you could answer the question, 'How can an artist make a living?'" Perhaps he too remembered their first evening spent with his family, but Reuben was ready to move on, and she was unable to tell him that she had written on exactly that topic. Instead he said, "Oh. Good. The bar is opening. We've time for a quick one. The preview starts at seven. Do you want to go?"

"Yes, I do. My mind is darting all over the place and it would be good to be distracted. It could be the beginning of the next stage of my artistic education!"

Reuben was taking Tansy to an exhibition that everyone was talking about and which he realised, now that she was a budding journalist, was one she should see. When they arrived Reuben noticed a large display of flyers for all the attractions that were on offer during the year. "We'll grab a few of those on our way out," he suggested.

"It's as if I have the job already," Tansy joked.

As students they had discounted tickets. "We better make the most of these too," Reuben said as he held their cards at the kiosk. "It's going to be a shock paying full price."

The exhibition was showing two contemporary artists and a sculptor. Reuben and Tansy wandered through the rooms, neither making a comment. He remembered how intimidated he felt on his first visit to an exhibition by the soundless floors, the air of reverence that pervaded the room, and the unblinking stares of the custodians. There were not many viewers. Reuben guided Tansy from one exhibit to another.

On their way out Tansy was silent.

"Was it okay? You weren't bored?" Reuben asked.

"That wasn't what I expected! I feared you would ask me what I thought."

"No point in that, it's art."

"What do you mean?" Tansy asked.

"You only have to look. You feel, but don't need to say anything."

"I might in an article."

"In that case you can say whatever comes into your head

at the time. It is purely your opinion because you are not an expert. It's like wine. A crowd of people taste the same wine. They all describe it differently, but the connoisseurs know the jargon."

"That's a bit harsh isn't it?" Tansy said.

"Not really. They taste so much wine, or in the case of art critics, they see so many pictures that they develop a language to describe their impressions, but they still can't tell you how you taste or feel. So your job is easy. Write what you feel. As I said, you will learn," Reuben responded.

"How do you know this?"

"How do you think? Years with my Dad. You will be able to write, you've been doing so for four years."

Reuben and Tansy turned off the street into a park which led towards Tansy's flat. "I am looking forward to July," she said thoughtfully. "I've had enough of being a student."

"July is my Dad's least favourite month. He says it's all that uniform green, that July is the only month when there is little variation in colour in nature."

"What sort of painting does he do? The paintings on the walls in your house are your mother's aren't they?"

"Dad's need more space. He paints now in a style that is a mixture of Braque and Cézanne and puts on the paint like Gauguin or van Gogh," Reuben teased. "You'll have to ask him next time you visit. Are you coming at the weekend?"

"Probably," Tansy hesitated. She removed her hand from Reuben's. "It depends on my flat. Whether to keep it."

"What do you mean?"

They were walking beside each other and Reuben could not see her face but he stopped and turned her towards him. "What is the matter?"

"What about after the summer? Where are you going to live next year? I'm wondering what you are doing for a flat. Do you want to share mine?" she asked, embarrassed.

Reuben put his arms around her. "One day, but not yet," he said, and felt Tansy relax.

"I'm so glad. I wasn't ready either."

Reuben kept hold of her hand as they continued along the pavement. "That's sorted then. Are you coming home with me this weekend?"

FOUR

"Do you think you are making the most of this space?"

The student looked over his shoulder, one hand poised with a hammer and the other holding a nail positioned to keep a canvas stretched over its frame.

"The examiners will enter from here, as I have done, and they will stop for a first impression. What will it be? Remember, artists deal in light as well as form and colour and all the other components that you know." Gerald gave the student time to take this in. "Do you think that the position of your display stand needs changing?"

"Probably," the student answered doubtfully.

"You have been here three years! I don't intend to tell you anything. What was your reason for placing the screens as they are?"

"To make you look. So you're not distracted by the window."

"How have you achieved that?" By now a group had gathered around Gerald, each anxious to hear his advice knowing that their turn to be assessed was to come.

"Has he achieved it?" Gerald swept his eyes over the group but none of them ventured an opinion.

"It might, or might not, help," Gerald hesitated, "to use the light instead of avoiding it."

He moved to the next student. "Is it important in which

order I look at your work?" he asked her. Gerald continued from one display to another, dropping a comment, a suggestion, giving a wry smile but never an indication of whether he liked or disliked their work.

He thought about his own work. How would it stand up to external scrutiny, he wondered. He had departed long ago from the simplistic style of his student days, so what was the point of a show? One student might produce copious amounts of work, but did that mean that the student was more deserving of a degree than another whose screens merely held a few small paintings? What did the degree mean? It certainly did not guarantee a job. Did a student go to college and spend three years perfecting and naively exploring a few fundamental ideas, just to become a teacher? Gerald used to think of himself as an artist who taught, his teaching being the means of putting pennies in the bank so that he could paint, but he had to admit that it was some time since he had painted, and even longer since anyone had bought one of his paintings.

Fortunately he enjoyed the contact with the students, he was popular and he knew that he could extract good work from them. He was sensitive to any who were struggling and whether it was with their work or whether with problems which emanated from outside the college, the students soon found in Gerald a sympathetic teacher.

At the end of the session Gerald walked down the corridor and saw that the door to Andrew's office was open. The staff room projected over the estuary, where the high tide covered the otherwise dreary mud and the early May sun glinted off the water, giving the room the feeling of a conservatory that was the envy of many another college. Although there were design faults which were to be expected from any new building – the graphics department grumbled about the poor lighting and the animation department about the lack of space – the fine arts had few complaints. The studios were large and well lit, and the staff room which Gerald entered was positioned in the prime position in the centre of the building.

Andrew was holding a mug of coffee and leaning against the radiator.

"Come in, Gerald!" Gerald could not suppress the feeling that he was still considered an unknown quantity by the principal. It was not only that Andrew had an easy authority but he had the confidence of someone who belonged. Andrew was a local boy who went away to pursue his career and then returned to capture one of the most prestigious posts in the district. A handsome man, his soft brown hair showed no signs of greying, he had a boyish face, kept a trim figure and, being athletic, moved gracefully. He always wore a long-sleeved shirt in checks or stripes and trend-setting jeans. Gerald, to emphasise that he was the sole member of the senior staff to come from south of the border, dressed more casually.

"Degree year working well?" Andrew asked, waving his mug to indicate that Gerald should make himself a coffee.

Gerald gave a shrug. "Same as usual. Trying to extract gold from a mixed bag of offerings. You'll know. They are not doing badly."

"The powers that be will be scrutinising us now the college is established."

"They'll be wanting value for money." Gerald filled the kettle.

Andrew nodded. "The paymasters will certainly be wanting to see some impressive results."

"And a good degree show will help our numbers and attract students from further afield. I appreciate your concern, Andrew, but I still have to work with the material I have."

"I am well aware of that. In fact some of the requirements that we are being asked to provide to maintain the same level of funding next year might ease the pressure on you."

Gerald defended his students and by inference his ability to draw out the best in them. "Andrew, they are quite capable of delivering the goods."

"I quite understand, and I have never doubted your skill, but the college is in its infancy. I worked hard to persuade the council to site the college here and I have ambitions for it. Imagine it rivalling St Ives!"

"That's hardly possible, St Ives has been around for years."

"I'm thinking of alternative ways in which we can promote our education here."

Gerald admired Andrew's drive and genuinely enjoyed teaching and working with the students, but he was forming his own ideas on how a college could thrive and feared that Andrew's plans might be superficial and cosmetic. "So, what are your plans?"

"They'll come up at the staff meeting. I'll put them to everyone, but I wanted to give you prior warning. I rely on your support, Gerald. I also value your contribution. You can be certain of that or why would you be one of my senior staff?"

There was a hesitant tap on the door.

"Ah, Callum."

Gerald was always pleased to see Callum. Reticent at meetings and willing to agree to any proposal that Andrew or he, as deputy, implemented, Callum supplied a balm to the sometimes argumentative atmosphere of the staff room. Where there was practical work with the students Callum managed well, provided that he was not expected to address a roomful of students. It was painful to see how uncomfortable he was when obliged to speak out. Gerald perched on the edge of the desk and Callum remained by the door.

"Let's sit." Andrew went over to his office chair and the two members of staff took the chairs on the opposite side of the desk.

Gerald sensed a change in the atmosphere as Andrew picked up a form from his desk and waved it. "This is interesting. Jacob's daughter's applying for art college. It would be quite a catch if she came here. You know, raise our profile. We might finally persuade Jacob to join our ranks."

"I don't know the man, but it seems that you haven't managed to entice him here yet," Gerald remarked.

"It might encourage Jacob to be less of a recluse," Callum commented when he saw Andrew looking to him for support. They had known one another since childhood.

Gerald saw the look and felt excluded. "I'm confused. If the man's a recluse, how does that help us? I've heard his name but he's hardly a Riley or a Damien Hirst. I can't say I've even seen his work. So why the interest?"

"You'll find Jacob is much respected around here. He doesn't actively promote or sell his work but he's immersed in paint. He has a way of seeing that he wants us to share, but it is more important for him to explore the physicality of painting. Those of us who know him think that we understand."

"Isn't it a bit arrogant, thinking that all he has to do is paint and somehow his work will be noticed and some ill-defined person will promote it?"

He could see Andrew bristle. "You don't understand. Jacob's leading the life that suits him. Fame and fortune don't feature. Hard as it is to comprehend, not all artists aspire to be exposed to scrutiny and possible lionisation by an adoring public. Jacob's a private man who's achieved an ideal that others only fantasise about, namely, back to mother nature and the pursuit of the power of paint."

Callum suggested, "Jacob seems to have some notion that college, where so many unformed minds are assembled together, is not helpful and could in practice drive away imagination."

"I am surprised he's allowing his daughter to apply," Gerald commented.

"Why shouldn't he? There is little he can do to stop her," Andrew said mildly. "I have no scruples in encouraging her. It will be to Jacob's advantage for her to study here. No maintenance costs."

"And Jacob can monitor her," Gerald added with mild sarcasm. "There are plenty of talented students to choose from. I still do not understand why you are so focused on Jacob's daughter."

When Gerald left to attend to his next class, Callum remained behind. Andrew stood for a few moments and gazed across the estuary. He suspected that his unease about Jacob's work being so neglected was the reason that he was anxious for his daughter to choose their college. Perhaps he might be able to give Jacob an opening to promote his work, and if Jacob did gain recognition, it would reflect well on his college. He wondered if Callum felt a similar loyalty towards Jacob, even if he did not share his ambition.

"Callum, you know Jacob," he spoke without turning from his contemplation of the scene through the window.

"He was an outstanding artist, even when we were students together. He has developed in a way that you only see in a dedicated artist." Callum ran his hand through his thinning sand-coloured hair.

Andrew wondered if he was embarrassed. "You spoke up on his behalf, I appreciate that it was hard for you." He did not expect Callum to answer. "The girl's going out with

John's son. You might drop a word. John can be persuasive when he puts his mind to it."

"If I can get hold of him! This is prime fishing season," Callum reminded him, "you could bend his ear yourself."

"Probably better coming from you," Andrew urged.

***

The harbour was like a magnet to Callum. Not more than five hundred yards from the college, the small port was home to a dwindling but active fleet of fishing vessels. If he needed a walk it was the water that beckoned, especially when there was something on his mind, as there was that day. He had misgivings about mixing friendship with his work at the college, and was undecided whether to broach the subject of Jacob's daughter's application with John.

Callum did not seek solitude, he was rarely alone on his walks along the estuary and had nodding acquaintances with many of the fishermen. The regular dog walkers and people taking exercise were familiar to him.

"Finished for the day?" an elderly man asked as they passed each other.

"Preparing for tomorrow!" Callum answered, their usual exchange.

Callum stood for a while and watched two children sitting on the wall play-acting fishing. He remembered the rod and line that he made with a long stick, some string and a bent clip, before being given his first real rod. John knew where to fish, and how, and that was when they began to spend hours together along the estuary. The tide moves fast, the water has a long journey to the sea and back, and there was excitement in timing their return so as to avoid being trapped in the exposed mud.

Callum followed the harbour wall. When the tide was

high there was a flurry of activity as boats sailed, moored, or prepared to cast off. The boat tied up below him had been neglected for some months, its owner now frail, and there seemed to be no buyer.

"You would think that his son would be taking to the sea. Spruce up the old boat." Callum stopped beside the speaker, a fisherman. "I'd take it on, but it's all I can do to keep a crew myself."

"It's a tough life. The young are not interested in making a living this way any more, it is too precarious."

"It has to be in the blood. It was in mine. You can't do it otherwise." Nodding to Callum as if to exonerate anyone who decided to choose another life, the fisherman gazed across the estuary.

Callum looked for John's boat. It was not at its usual mooring, a large fishing boat was in its place. A movement rocked the deck, and a burly man with a tanned face emerged from the cabin. Callum lifted a hand in greeting.

"Good evening." A foreigner, but Callum could not place the accent. He wondered what the man would think of their little harbour, with only a fish and chip shop and a café selling ice creams in the car park.

He walked past several pleasure boats before seeing another of the regular fishermen who was working on his engine.

"Good catch?" he called, and on seeing Callum the fisherman grinned.

"It was last night! Tides high at six. Weather forecast is promising. What are you up to? You teachers have the life of Riley!"

"I'm the first to admit it. You know that!"

Abandoned boats lay on the bank, some in a reasonable condition and still able to be restored. Callum used to think that he would do up one of them when he retired, but as he got older the attraction lessened. He would enjoy the reconstruction, but he began to see that it was mere fantasy. He would not have the necessary skill, nor the stamina, to go out to sea.

"Seems a waste, all these redundant boats," Callum commented.

"Pipe dreams?" the fisherman retorted.

"Not any more!

"I'm on my way to see John. He'll be sailing tonight too, I reckon."

John's boat was moored where the path narrowed, *St Ninian* painted along her side. The rope curled around the bollard and was fastened neatly. Callum admired the ease with which John completed the rituals of tying up or casting off. Perhaps he should sit here in the summer and paint. His paintings were not ambitious, local landscapes or seascapes, but he wanted to capture the timeless quality that this scene portrayed. He gave a tug on the rope.

"Hello," he called, treading carefully as he descended the seaweed covered steps.

John emerged from the galley. "Have a beer," he offered, "I'm sorting out some charts."

Callum stepped over the rail on to the deck and followed John down into the cabin.

Spread out over the table were several charts, well thumbed from constant use. John switched easily from meticulous skipper to relaxed companion. With quick decisive movements he folded the charts, placed them in their pigeon-hole and, bending over to open a locker, retrieved two cans. His wiry, muscular frame was indicative of a man whose every action was economical.

Callum sat on the bench against the wall and ran his hand along the smooth edge of the table. The craftsmanship displayed in the interior of boats surpassed any that he had seen on shore: the neat lockers, each with their catches, the galley, a kitchen in miniature and yet providing for every eventuality. On board, with space at a premium, and security from displacement on the seas a vital consideration, efficient arrangements for essentials were a priority. He appreciated, as an artist, the beauty inherent in objects which were made with only their function as a guide.

"Coming to the TT races this year?" John asked.

John usually invited Callum on the four-day annual trip to the Isle of Man and it was a date that was fixed in the calendar. John passed up the profits from fishing to entertain his friends by sailing to the Isle for the TT races. Although he had never ridden a motorcycle, not even pillion, Callum found the races thrilling, and he enjoyed the camaraderie of the group.

He felt pleasure tinged with relief. He did not presume on his invitation each year and answered with a nonchalance he did not feel. "I'd like that." He looked around the cabin and through the open door to the interior and sleeping quarters. "Not for the world would I do your job," he remarked.

John gave him a grin. "And not for the world would I do yours. Dealing with useless students all day would send me crazy."

"Why useless?"

"What will any of them do with an art degree? You tell me. It's just a cop out, dabbling in pottery and paint. Now, computer graphics I could understand, but art, what sort of job do they really think it will lead to?"

Callum was used to this sort of discussion and let John continue. "Ninety per cent of them will do something else, and a few might teach. Sorry Callum! I just don't see it!"

"What about the ten per cent, or even one per cent,

there has to be a place for them. It's not just art, the same can be said for music and dance."

"There are orchestras and bands for music students for which they get paid. Dancers are able to get work in clubs and cruise ships, but with your lot, no one is going to pay them to paint."

"Sure, patrons of art were a phenomenon in the past, except in rare incidences, but even then the artist had to be established and commissions did not leave the artist free to paint original work."

"Tell me, Callum, did people buy your work?"

Callum laughed ruefully. "Why do you think I am teaching? Yes, I wanted to be the iconic artist but being penniless did not suit. I might return to it one day, you can't resist its pull if it is in you." He took up his beer can and gave a sweep with his arm. "Your life is all work, John. What would you do if you could?"

"Not much time to think about it. Enjoy terra firma, the garden, you know." When at home he spent all his hours there. Callum admired his knowledge of plants and marvelled at how he kept his lawns mown and landscaped with shrubs and trees while at the same time spending hours at sea.

"I'm curious about McFarlane's," John said. "Do you still get the numbers? I mean do you still get plenty of students applying?"

"The numbers stay steady. At their age all they know is that they need some sort of degree and many do not discriminate about which subject they choose. Few of them have any idea what they want from life, and they know even less what jobs might be available for them."

"It comes down to work! Damned hard work and don't let them think otherwise. Student life is too easy and no preparation for a real job. I started on the boats at sixteen.

The hours were long, the conditions tough and the discipline strict but if you could cope there were good rewards. It makes us fishermen intolerant of landsmen!"

Callum appreciated how fortunate he was. "I know I have a good deal. I used to spend long hours on lengthy commutes and diminished living space. I've done my bit."

"City life would be an anathema to me."

While they finished their beers John cleared the draining board, stowed the crockery, and then rinsed out the cans. "I'll walk back with you."

They fell into step, followed the row of bollards to the end of the quay, and then turned up the road leading towards the town. It was quiet at this time of day. Tourists and shoppers had dispersed for their evening meals. This was how Callum liked it. Nothing seemed to have changed since their boyhood. This was how it had been when he had drifted down to the harbour, usually alone, and imagined the adventures of ships going to sea. He remembered seeing John, his satchel flapping against his legs, running after school along the deserted high street to the waterfront to join his grandfather. It was simple nostalgia because the small fishing town had always been a famous attraction for holiday-makers and the harbour a hub of activity, but John had been so intent on reaching his grandfather and became so engrossed in the tasks he was set that he was oblivious of anyone else.

Through John, Callum learnt the contentment found in the outdoors and this may have contributed to his solitary existence, yet he still craved companionship, and the trip to the Isle of Man was the highlight of his year. However, he had a subject other than the forthcoming trip to introduce.

"We have an interesting prospective student." He was not surprised that John stopped for a moment and turned towards him.

"At college? What do you mean?" he asked.

"It's Abi. Jacob's daughter. She's applied."

"David never told me!" John answered, puzzled. "Perhaps she hasn't told him."

"Andrew wondered if perhaps David had persuaded her, so that she could be near him. From what we understand Jacob has some notion that art college is not for his children."

"Does Jacob know?"

"We are not sure. Andrew has always wanted to have him involved with the college. He is convinced that Jacob's work will eventually be universally recognised and that association with him would help our profile. On the other hand, having his daughter as a student, should Jacob's work take off, would be a feather in our cap."

"It seems unlikely that Abi has told David."

"Neither of us can say anything then." Callum was not going to risk breaking Andrew's confidence any further. He had only promised to speak to John. "But if the subject were to surface, we'd be keen to have her."

John nodded, understanding.

"To be honest, John, no college, not even McFarlane's, is immune from cuts, but one way of avoiding scrutiny is to keep a high profile and a healthy number of student applicants. I have a vested interest in its survival. The lifestyle suits me and I've no wish to move or seek another post. It's difficult to explain why I'm content to teach art and merely create small works of my own. I've no particular drive to make my mark. I fervently believe that the world is enriched by artists and when I influence one or two talented young people in their careers I feel that my time is not wasted. Besides, when again in their life can someone indulge in creativity to the extent that a college course allows?"

John pulled his collar up, the wind was increasing, but Callum anticipated a counter-argument.

"Life is not about self-indulgence, but it can be assumed that Abigail, at least, has talent. I like the girl." They began walking again, heads down. "It seems natural that she would want to follow in her father's footsteps. What I don't understand is why she doesn't want to strike out for herself. Get out of her father's shadow."

"Could be financial. You know, the cost of living away from home is a great burden." Callum did not like to mention that he only partly believed this.

"There's nothing to stop her earning her keep and getting a job. She'd still have time."

"To dabble in art?" Callum finished the sentence for him and smiled. "I'll not take offence, John."

"I'm not certain that having a girl on shore will make it any easier for David when he starts with my crew."

Callum stopped as their paths diverged and waited for his verdict. John reached forward and gave Callum's shoulder a friendly slap. "I'll not put a spanner in the works!"

FIVE

"How did anyone land a fish that size?" This was not the first time that Reuben had asked himself this question. Across from where he was polishing glasses hung a twenty-five-pound salmon mounted on a wooden frame. Alongside displays of fly ties with their delicate feathers and gruesome hooks, the salmon was one of several mounted fish that had been caught locally, preserved by a taxidermist, and below which were plaques stating the weight, date and the name of the fishermen. "How difficult it must be to preserve the skin and eyes and to stuff them with sawdust." Reuben placed the glass on a shelf so that it aligned with its neighbour and selected another from the sink that was hidden beneath the counter. "At least the meat was not wasted. How many would twenty pounds of fish feed?"

Someone was trying to catch his attention. "A pint of bitter?" Reuben repeated hopefully, and it was late enough that the customer was oblivious to the particular brand of alcohol so long as his glass was refilled.

Reuben had worked at the King's Arms since he was sixteen, when he was allocated to the kitchen, spending four hours at a stretch with his hands in water too hot for comfort. From here he progressed to waiting at table until he was eligible to be introduced to the mysteries of the bar. There were more varieties of whisky than could fill one shelf and they overflowed to join the gins, sherries and a disconcerting number of liqueurs. It was not sufficient merely to be able to read the labels, since their pronunciation often bore no relation to the logical unravelling of the letters. Learning a foreign language had been an easy task when compared with mastering the language of liquor.

During the winter months Reuben knew the local customers and the job was routine. At this time of the year new faces began to appear as tourists returned and the pace of work increased, resulting in a longer spell at the end of the day. At this point in the evening the bar was emptying and Reuben could begin to clear and clean up without having to respond jovially to every order.

When he described his childhood to Tansy he had painted only part of the picture; the time until he left school and began to support himself. For her he relived the games they played and the expeditions they undertook. He wondered at first if she would understand the exhilaration and sense of discovery that they found in the countryside when all her experiences had been of overseas holidays and organised trips, but she soon became engrossed in his storytelling.

At some distance from their house, but within easy reach by bicycle, lived their friends. Younger sisters rode on the crossbar as their older siblings pedalled along single-track roads. Every year the large dam which they had constructed to create a swimming hole was repaired and lined with sheets of plastic to contain the water. It might be the summer but the temperature could be cool, and the water in the burn even colder.

When they were tired of that game they waded down the burn to where it joined the river. They knew the pool where the salmon hid and would try their hand at tickling. Rarely did they land a fish.

One year a rope was slung around a branch overhanging

a pool at a bend in the river. Each child was dared to grab the rope and swing out, releasing it when they were above the deepest part of the pool, and none refused.

On other days the older boys would set up ramps and an obstacle course, urging each other to tackle ever more ambitious jumps. Reuben remembered injuring his ankle severely enough to warrant a visit to the doctor.

And then there were the expeditions, the whole family kitted out in wellington boots and various layers of clothes depending on the time of year, with a vast picnic. Setting off through the woods of snowdrops, daffodils or bluebells if it was early in the year, or darkened and eerie from the leafy covering in summer, they headed for the hill. The climb was strenuous but from the top the children surveyed their whole world. In winter they sledged and in summer they rolled down the grass, and nothing compared to the sensation of conquering the summit.

Their favourite haunt was the scramble down the glen burn where they were so near to a popular walk but so hidden that it was their secret alone. They started at the rock which they called the Castle. Handing their clothes to their parents, invariably shivering, they stood on top of the granite slab contemplating the peat-coloured water as it gushed alongside, creating a pool below. They lowered themselves and began to swim and then scramble. The exhilaration of discovering the next pool or negotiating awkward boulders spurred them on and kept the momentum until they reached their goal: a twelve-foot-high waterfall which cascaded into a perfectly round pool. If you braved the water, for by now fingers were white and lips were blue, you could swim to the ledge behind the waterfall, let the icy water run over your hand and hide behind its curtain. At this point in his story Reuben had looked at Tansy to see if she grasped any of the magic.

Slightly bemused she said, "It wasn't like that where I lived." But after a short while she added, "Perhaps you could take me there one day?"

He recalled for her only the years before his father's exhibition. Prior to that event, although he was aware that no one else had parents who were painters, he had not considered it of any consequence. What occupied him and his friends was fishing, football, the latest new song and generally mucking about. Reuben was convinced, now, that the attitude of his friends did not change, but his own did. Deciding to take his exams and to leave school early, by the following summer he was working full-time.

Partly because his work schedule prevented him from socialising, but partly by choice, he began to alienate himself from his friends. His brush with the cruel reality of attempting to earn a living outside a conventional career sobered him, maturing him at a faster rate than his contemporaries. He knew that the more serious outlook that he took on life irritated his friends and he found it easier to avoid conflict. Eventually, after he had been at university for several months, he found a group of friends with whom he felt in tune. That intervening period had been a lonely time, but Reuben realised that he benefitted from the isolation and evolved a template by which he now lived his life. Although open-minded as to where his career would lead, a sound financial training was essential to prevent the family from suffering unnecessary hardship in the future.

If he became a little more distant and argumentative, they accepted that as part of the new influences on his life. In reality he was driving a wedge between his bohemian home, which he began to see as unrealistic, and his adoption of a career path towards earning a substantial income. Perhaps it had been going to the other extreme to enter the financial sector, which required a facility and an interest in the abstract world of figures and how they relate to commodities. In comparison to his childhood environment, it was curious that he had embarked on this career in finance, but prospects for promotion were good and there seemed no reason at present to question the decision.

Reuben took a cloth, submerged it into the soapy water and wrung it out. He could hear the clatter of plates in the kitchen as they were stacked and the intermittent slam of the door of the fridge as food was stored. No one spoke at the end of the night, all keen to 'red up' and head for home. He went around the side of the bar and, beginning at the furthermost table, cleared beer mats and wiped the surfaces.

That evening his concern was for Abigail. Four years his junior, he felt protective towards her, especially as she had voiced her determination to develop her undoubted talent as an artist. Moreover she seemed immovable in her decision to apply to the new college that had been established in the town and she seemed to be resistant to any discussion.

On the bus home Reuben tried to clarify his underlying misgivings. As the daughter of a locally renowned artist, Abigail carried the burden of high expectation. Although the work of a student did not attract the same level of scrutiny as that received at an exhibition, she would be vulnerable. He feared that undue criticism might break her spirit in much the same way as his father's disastrous foray into the commercial field had affected his own.

When he let himself into the house Tansy was the only one awake.

"It's good of you to wait up," he said gratefully. He sank to the sofa beside her and she put her head on his shoulder.

"Still worrying?" she asked.

"About Abi? Yes. How am I to find out if the staff are of a sufficiently high calibre to be entrusted with my sister's talent?"

"Why wouldn't the college attract good teachers? There's no reason to assume otherwise," Tansy attempted to reassure him. "You have to trust that your sister's drive and conviction in her own ability will carry her through and if she lives at home it will give her a safe base."

"If I was sensible I would stop worrying. After all it is out of our hands." Tansy turned her head and gave a suspicion of a nod. Reuben drew her face towards him knowing that he should act on his words.

"There is always the possibility that the college will reject her application."

***

Reuben was going with David to collect a second-hand car. He asked Tansy if she minded staying at the cottage, and she answered that she certainly did not want to go buying cars. Her motivation was a conversation that had taken place between her and Jacob. He had asked Tansy in what area of journalism she was planning to work. When Tansy explained she expected, even from the courteous Jacob, some mildly caustic remark, but he had merely commented that she had better come over to the mill sometime. Tansy hoped that this would give her an opportunity to do so.

"Tansy, are you free to spend time with me?" Matty asked while they were in the kitchen eating breakfast. "Can I show you my room, and perhaps you can help with my homework?" Tansy was unused to young people but was flattered by Matty's attention.

"Tansy might have other things she wants to do," Deborah said and gave Tansy a questioning look. Tansy was touched. "I'd love to do that," she told Matty, but at the same time thought that Florrie might feel ignored and made a mental note to seek her out during the morning.

Matty's room was small, with a single bed, desk and chair, and was simply furnished. It had none of the electronic gadgets that you might expect a twelve-year-old to own. Instead, her desk was covered with books, paper and craft materials. There was a much-hugged teddy on her bed and on the walls, attached with drawing pins, were paintings in a variety of mediums. There was a neat row of shoes in one corner consisting of two pairs of well-worn trainers, leather lace-ups for school and a pair of snug fluffy ankle-high slippers. "I got those for Christmas," Matty said, pointing, "They are delicious."

"What are you drawing?" Tansy asked.

Matty extracted a piece of folded A4 paper from under her drawing pad. "Making a card for Mummy's birthday. I've done the drawing and now it's ready to be painted." She handed the card to Tansy. The drawing was of the cottage as it had looked earlier in the year. Leafless trees formed a stark background of interlacing branches, beneath which the cottage was a peaceful haven. Matty had depicted the slate roof, deep-set wooden, paned windows and the arch of the porch in meticulous detail. She had faithfully drawn all the many clumps of snowdrops which filled the border surrounding the house with neat pencil strokes.

Tansy thought she had captured the timeless quality of her home. "This is lovely," Tansy commented and Matty's eyes shone. "How are you going to paint all this, all these window panes and flower heads, and the individual bricks?"

"I know. It is difficult. I think I'll draw the outline in ink and then use watercolours. It will take a while because you have to allow the paint to dry between each new colour."

"She will be thrilled." Still holding the card, Tansy then studied the pictures pinned to the wall where the same style of drawing, with attention to detail and lightness of touch, was also evident. They gave Tansy a feeling of optimism that she could not completely analyse. "These are all yours?"

"They are old ones. Shall I show you my art folder? That's what I call this pile. It's so that I can be ready for art school."

Tansy and Matty spent some time discussing each picture. "If they are not good they're not allowed in my folder," Matty informed Tansy emphatically. "Dad told me to start going outside to draw, that's why I did the cottage. When I go to college I won't stay here like Abi. I'll go far away from home and no one will know who I am and I'll be able to paint what I want."

Tansy wondered if this was intuition on Matty's part or whether Abigail had confided in her. Tansy felt that this was an opportune moment to encourage Matty to study elsewhere. "Going to new places is often very helpful."

Tansy had struck a chord. Matty answered thoughtfully, "You've visited a lot of places, haven't you? I mean, you had to, if you were brought up in Africa, you would have to leave home to study."

Tansy smiled, but did not contradict. "I could have studied anywhere, but I chose here. Just as you can choose one day."

Matty took back the card and sat down at her desk. She opened her paint-box and selected a brush and as Tansy watched Matty, absorbed already in her project, she envied the young girl and wished that she had a correspondingly creative impulse.

Downstairs Florrie was playing the piano.

"Can I come and listen?" Tansy asked tentatively, standing at the doorway of the living room. Florrie did not stop playing but nodded her head rapidly. The piece was by Liszt. Tansy had taken piano lessons until serious exam revision had usurped all her free time so she recognised the piece. She sat in one of the armchairs out of Florrie's line of sight.

Florrie was more than proficient and played the piece to the end before pushing back her piano stool, and, allowing her shoulders to drop, turned towards Tansy with her face flushed.

Tansy suspected that Florrie would distrust her if she made a great demonstration of approval, instead she said simply, "Florrie, I enjoyed that very much."

"I've still some phrasing to practise and there are two bars I always struggle with," Florrie's words were tumbling out breathlessly. "I haven't played this piece to anyone before. I'm glad you liked it."

"What other piece are you learning?"

"A Scarlatti but I'm not ready yet to play it to you."

"Have you any other piece that I could hear?"

"I could play part of a Beethoven sonata if you like."

Tansy sat back in her chair, delighted that she would play again. Florrie lifted the lid of the piano stool to find the music. She seemed to be as absorbed in her music as Matty had been in her drawing. This gifted family had a unique ability to cultivate their talents, influenced, no doubt, by watching their parents, and as a result lived in an atmosphere where creativity took the place of electronic games. Tansy made a mental note to include these observations in her next article.

When she had finished playing, Florrie chose a chair opposite Tansy. "Do you play?" she asked.

"Not any more. Are you going to make music your career?"

"I don't think so. I'm not good enough for solo playing and I don't want to teach. One thing I do know is that I don't want to go to college." She said this fiercely and looked with a challenge at Tansy.

"You mean art college. Do you draw?"

"I can. I used to a lot, but with such competition in the house I gravitated to music."

"So why are you against college?"

Before she could answer Deborah came through the open door. "Tansy, you wanted to see Jacob's paintings. He said to ask if you were free."

In the kitchen Jacob said, "I'll show you the garden first." Then noticing Tansy's shoes he added, "You'll need boots. Let's see if I can find a pair to fit you."

Tansy was not sure if Jacob was irritated by her request or whether he was indifferent. The wellington boots, far from being in neatly paired rows, were in an untidy pile beneath the coat hooks. Jacob chose two that could have been a pair, upturned each boot and shook them, tapping the soles, and watched a few flakes of dried grass fall out. "Always best to check," he commented, "in the winter the mice can nest in them if they are left for any length of time." When she put her feet into the boots the unexpected cold and the unforgiving material were novel sensations. Then she remembered that she must have worn boots as a child, in the park, and their association was always pleasant, but these, unlike her shiny flower-patterned childhood boots, were utilitarian black and caked with mud.

It was a dull morning and, typical of coastal areas, the air was laden with water without actually raining. On every blade of grass or outstretched leaf rested a film of water.

Tansy followed Jacob to the wooden shed. Like the house, it had seen better days. The roof was covered in moss and the wood was bleached and grooved with age. The door dropped on its hinges as Jacob opened it to reach for a fork. The pebble path along which they walked glistened and the earth on either side was a deep sandy brown. Sections of the stone dyke surrounding the garden had collapsed and temporary fencing had been devised using old gates and wire.

"We have a problem with rabbits. The wall needs mending, as you can see, but there are always more jobs pending than time allows."

Jacob led Tansy through to a part of the garden which had been tilled and where mounds of soil were raised into rows. At regular intervals were tall leafy potato plants, some with small yellow flowers, some with purple. Jacob reached out to remove a few flower heads.

"I have been told that if you pinch out the flowers the plants yield a better crop."

Jacob led Tansy through another gate to the orchard. Beneath the trees the grass grew unchecked and on the branches embryo fruits were forming. For a while Jacob stood and gazed. "It's a beautiful sight in spring. Don't underestimate the power of beauty! That tree over there has wonderful cookers, they melt when boiled and are perfect for crumbles."

Tansy went across to one of the trees, and taking off one of her gloves, touched the bark. She turned to look at Jacob and smiled, "What about this one?"

"I nearly cut it down," Jacob admitted. "It had produced nothing for years, and now look at it! It's much the same with artists. Fallow for months and then an explosion of activity."

"Don't you have to paint every day?"

"Not now." Jacob thought for a moment. "In the early years, you are right. You need to paint or draw all the time even if some are discarded. You can't produce a masterpiece every time."

"Is that why we need colleges?" Tansy asked mischievously.

Jacob laughed. "Good girl!" Tansy blushed. "To my mind regular drawing should start years earlier. Children should be drawing and getting guidance and not just one art lesson a week. It's like practising scales and arpeggios on a piano. Painters need the tools of their trade and only practice will hone their pencil or brush skills and only time spent experimenting will perfect their choice of colours."

He led Tansy towards the mill and then stood by the gate.

"They need to look at the work of others. Feast their eyes on the Old Masters, the Cubists, the Impressionists, and see how they achieved their effects. History of art is important."

Jacob stopped suddenly. "Sorry. I get carried away."

Tansy no longer felt uncomfortable. "It's interesting, do go on."

"First let me show you the rest of the garden since you're all kitted up. This is rhubarb." Tansy ran her hand over the large rough-edged, crumpled leaves of the rhubarb and saw the thick pink and green stalks hidden beneath them.

"The pink stalks are the ones that are ready to be picked. We'll take some in to Deborah." He bent down and grasped a stalk close to the base of the plant and then gave Tansy a brief nod. "Your turn!"

Tansy chose carefully and then eased the rhubarb stalk until it came away, revealing a spoon-shaped indentation where it had been attached. As she searched for further stalks she wondered if Jacob could have any inkling of the excitement that she felt at being introduced to real paintings by a real artist. Jacob took the bunch and placed it on a shelf inside the scullery door.

It was only a short distance from the door of the scullery to the mill. The building was rectangular, had a slate roof and was constructed of rough stone which would have been unremarkable but for the profusion of Virginia creeper that had covered the walls and tried to obscure the windows. It was clear that Jacob had cut back the creeper and cleared it from the gutters, but otherwise it had been allowed to grow unchecked. On the outside of the building were stone steps to an upper level, but Tansy made her way to a door at ground level which was ajar.

The entrance was dark and was used for storage of miscellaneous gardening tools; however, light fell from an upper window on a wooden staircase which Tansy proceeded to climb. Propped upright against the wall, immediately opposite the top stair, was a large painting. Before Tansy could do more than register its impact, Jacob was heading towards a stack of paintings at one end of the room. "That's one of my most recent paintings. You'd do best to start by looking at my early ones. Come along!"

Tansy followed Jacob across the bare wooden floor. It was covered with a film of dust, which did not scatter under their feet but stuck to the surface. Four windows along the right side and two along the left filled the room with natural light. Canvasses were placed in groups against the walls. Reuben had told her that Jacob's work was held in esteem by other artists, and she felt ill-informed and out of her depth; nothing so far had prepared her for this encounter. She was apprehensive that she might not like what she saw and would not be able to hide her opinion, even while knowing that her appreciation or lack of it was probably immaterial to Jacob.

He started by turning over painting after painting from a pile in the furthermost corner. With conflicting emotions assailing her, Tansy was delighted that these works were representational and their subjects recognisable. She inferred from her glimpse of the painting at the head of the stairs that Jacob's work had developed towards the abstract.

She stood absorbed as Jacob showed her canvas after canvas, taking her on a journey. The colours were strong and in oil, but they were not garish. Gradually the shapes became less recognisable and yet she still felt that she had not lost touch with his depiction of the land and the sea.

Jacob did not ask Tansy any questions, nor did she feel obliged to make comments. Reuben had told her that she only had to feel and she was glad for his advice. Any remark she might make would feel presumptuous. She was as excited as if she was being shown pieces in a treasure chest. She was not certain that she understood the contents but she hoped in time to learn.

Never before had she been in the presence of the author of a work of literature, music or art, of this calibre. She had expected to feel overwhelmed, but she had not expected to feel so privileged. It was as if she was entering a territory where the climate, customs and language were alien. She had no previous experience to draw on to enable her to process her reaction. She had watched the total immersion that gripped other viewers in galleries and did not comprehend the emotions that the paintings elicited. She guessed that they might evoke memories or that the subject matter might be important, or the manner in which the painter had applied the paint, juxtaposed the colours or composed the canvas, but now that Jacob had invited her to his studio she was eager to understand how a painter communicated.

She was intrigued that an artist was driven by the need to capture on paper a landscape, a still life or a portrait. She thought that she could understand a portrait, capturing the essence of a person that could not be achieved in the same way by a camera, but she was confused by the change from realism to abstract. The shift of reference eluded her. She concluded with the sombre thought that the viewer did not matter, only that the image visualised by the artist should be transferred to paper.

Finally Jacob lifted the canvas that she had passed at the top of the stairs and placed it in the centre of the room where it would benefit from the light. "Stand well back," Jacob instructed.

The colours in the upper half of the canvas were blocks of blue and black with the shape in the centre encircled by a partially blue and partially yellow halo. Stripes of pink, blue and yellow were surrounded by more black paint and shades of yellow overlapped at random to cover the lower half.

And then Tansy saw what Jacob had created; a girl walking towards them with the light behind her. The painting was serene in ambience and the movement of the girl was languid and slow. How could this all emanate from brush-strokes of paint?

For the first time Tansy looked directly at Jacob. He ran his hand over his beard, a gesture that did not disguise the contented twinkle in his eyes, as he saw in her expression a gleam of comprehension.

"There you have it." Jacob lifted the heavy canvas as if it was cardboard, and replaced it in its original position. He appeared to be reluctant to release Tansy. She was over-whelmed and made as if to go back down the stairs.

"I've been thinking," he said and Tansy turned and smiled questioningly. "I noticed that you listened to my cogitations on making a living as an artist." Tansy nodded. "If paintings can be owned only for a set amount of time, the answer is leasehold."

"And what is leasehold?"

"Leasehold is a contract where one person conveys property, in this instance a painting, for a specified period of time. Usually quite a long time. The new owner keeps the painting, but it can only be passed on, or leased on in this case, by the original owner. How about this for an idea?"

Jacob was challenging her and she was fascinated by the idea.

"Would people want to lease paintings?"

"Real art lovers will want to own a painting by whatever method is available," Jacob replied and this time Tansy understood that he was serious.

"To be an artist," Jacob began, and Tansy walked across to stand beside him where he was contemplating his current painting, "you need to be as whole and as human as you can. If you want to communicate, you have to have something to say."

Tansy was as affected by the charisma of Jacob's per-sonality as she was by the impact of his painting. She empathised with Reuben's frustration that his father's works were hidden from the public eye and resolved that she would endeavour to give Jacob's art the opportunity to gain the appreciation that it deserved.

"Thank you," Jacob said as they removed their boots, but as Tansy entered the kitchen she wondered whether she should not have been the one doing the thanking.

Holding the bunch of stalks with their large leaves still attached, Tansy handed the rhubarb like a trophy to Deborah.

Reuben was sitting at the kitchen table and was surprised to see Tansy with his father. "What have you been up to?"

"Having my eyes opened!" She sat down beside him.

"Indoctrinating Tansy, Dad?" Reuben teased.

SIX

To those on board John's fishing boat, the weather on the crossing to the Isle of Man was kind. The journey was completed in daylight, giving the five men time to spend the evening in Douglas prior to the start of the TT races the next day.

Andrew and Callum had been on all John's expeditions to the Isle and recently Craig, another childhood friend, had been a regular guest. All four had been at school together but John was the only one whose work kept him in their home town. His family had been fishermen for generations and his grandfather had been the first to purchase his own boat. When John's father had died young he had stepped into his shoes. He was ready to take over when his grandfather retired and had proved that he was more than capable, modernising the boat and adapting to the changing methods of fishing.

Craig was an antique dealer, but he had not always been in the trade; he had slipped into it until eventually it had become a full-time occupation. His wife Clare had a consultancy at the hospital and he no longer had need of a reliable income because their children were grown up and their mortgage paid off. He had lived in Edinburgh for all of his adult life and the thought of moving back home did not enter into his calculations, but his work was lonely and returning to his home town to sail to the Isle of Man for the annual TT race with John was an important occasion.

The trade was changing and Craig had sold his business as it did not support a shop. He operated through the internet while renting a small warehouse and rarely purchased items that were too large to fit into his estate car. With his optimism at full throttle, he maintained a quick turnover. Craig began to specialise in paintings and, practically, they were a commodity that was easy to handle. He had no aspirations to be an artist himself but he, Andrew and Callum had a good crack each year on John's boat, baiting each other over their respective professions. This year was no exception and as John skippered his friends across to the Isle, the banter flowed, augmented and encouraged by John's fourth passenger, Taylor. He, like Craig, professed that he had no artistic talent.

John's sister had died leaving her husband, Taylor, so he had gleaned from family members, adrift and distraught. John had always been somewhat in awe of his brother-in-law; successful as an insurance broker, he and his sister rarely visited since what spare time they had from their demanding jobs was spent on holidays abroad. When they had met, John found Taylor a reasonable man and could not think of his predicament without wanting to rectify the situation. He invited Taylor to join them this year and was surprised and delighted when Taylor accepted. "Sailing and motorbikes!" Taylor had said to John's proposal. "Both new to me, so probably a good idea. Besides, it's good of you to invite me, when do we set off?"

John's boat was moored in the centre of Douglas harbour and as it was where all the ferries arrived, the port was seething with activity. Bikes and motorbike enthusiasts were disgorged from the ferries until the pavements overflowed, the hotels booked to capacity and the cafés inundated with customers.

On his first trip to the Isle of Man, when he still had

his shop in Leith, Craig discovered Eoin, the owner of the sole antique shop on the island. The two men kept in touch and Craig never failed to find time to call in. The visits always extended longer than Craig intended but his friends knew that he would join them in his own time. Craig walked towards the upper end of the town where the crowds were thinner.

He stopped outside Eoin's shop. The exterior was badly in need of paint, the wooden sills needed replacing and his sign had faded almost to obscurity. Craig wondered if, since it added to the air of antiquity and proclaimed the charms of a lost world, Eoin left it like that on purpose but it was possible that business was not thriving. Craig hoped that it was not the latter.

He peered through the window. This at least was free of dust and the glass was clean. The objects on display were shiny and well-presented but Craig could not help feeling a touch of professional snobbery. Most of the items in the window had little intrinsic value and were there to attract the passing tourist, but he flattered himself that he could spot the one object of value which had been put amongst them to lure the discerning dealer in expectation of some collectors' items. A sign said 'open', but whether this was because Eoin was expecting him and not because he anticipated any trade, he could not be certain.

He pushed the door. The interior was particularly dismal and apart from the light coming in from the window nothing illuminated the room.

"Eoin. You there?" Craig called and Eoin appeared from a rear doorway, switching on a light as he did so.

"My good friend! Here again!" They gave each other a firm handshake. Craig beamed and Eoin waved an arm around the shop. "See if you can ferret out any of my recent discoveries. There aren't many. I'll fetch us some tea, no sugar?"

The place was much as he remembered it but Craig noticed that Eoin seemed to have shifted his emphasis. The walls now hung with shelves, where before they had been covered in paintings, and these displayed pewter and brass trinkets, ornaments, jugs and plates. Eoin still had a few choice pieces of furniture, small tables and desks, ornamental chairs and mirrors, because there was a market for these on the island, but the selection of silver items laid out on a couple of small round tables was new.

Eoin placed the two mugs on his desk and they sat on either side in what felt to both men like a timeless tradition.

Craig examined his friend. "Beard a bit whiter and hair a bit thinner, but you look good."

"I could say the same for you, without the beard."

"They've become quite fashionable."

Eoin stroked his beard slowly with a twinkle in his eye. "Me. Fashionable?"

"Never!" affirmed Craig who self-consciously ran his hand through his hair. When at work Craig dressed smartly in a three-piece suit, but on the island he wore his sailing gear; a top end waterproof jacket, Aran sweater and good quality trousers which served him well on the boat or on the island. In both situations the weather could turn nasty without warning.

"Trade good?" he asked. He gestured towards the wall where the paintings used to hang.

"Can't complain." Craig was relieved because the state of the shop did not reflect it but he nodded in agreement. His sales had been steady for a few years. "I see you've switched your interest."

"Ah! There's a story. I may be barking up the wrong tree, or I may be the canniest dealer in the business, but I've sold them. Took them to the mainland and, as you can see, bought pewter, brass and silver. They sell well by the way."

"What prompted this?" Craig sipped his tea and gazed past Eoin to appreciate a pretty pewter plate. Eoin had crazes when he decided that something would take off. He was usually right. On his small island where he was the sole dealer, variety was essential and he had a singular knack for judging the mood of his buyers.

"I've friends from all over the island and when they come to town they'll drop in, discuss things, try ideas on me, and one idea stuck."

Craig, alert to the possibility that he might pick up a tip or two, waited to be introduced to Eoin's current analysis of the market.

"There is a severe lack of money coming into the island. Tourist numbers are down, and those that visit are spending less. The housing market has gone slack so there is little income from that. We have a thriving banking system, as you know, but the benefit to the island is limited and financially it remains static. It has not increased for the last two years."

"I thought tourism was a good source of income."

"Yes, it's good but it isn't increasing and the island is going into debt."

"So how does that affect you?"

"I said, I got rid of my paintings."

"What has that to do with anything?" Craig said abruptly. Eoin was being obtuse.

"One of my friends is a member of the Isle's parliament, Tynwald, and he is also past curator of our prestigious national gallery. He is going to suggest that they sell their collection of Old Masters."

"But that is short-sighted, a one-off."

"Bear with me. He plans to introduce a law by which any painting that is over a hundred years old is owned by the state, our country."

"You mean confiscate them?"

"Effectively. All pictures over one hundred years old would lose their copyright, so to speak. No one can own them after that time, they become common property."

Craig looked at Eoin, uncomprehending. Eoin stood up and took a book from a shelf.

"This book. Imagine it is J. M. Barrie's *Peter Pan*. For one hundred years the royalties of every sale went to Great Ormond Street Hospital. They could have gone to Barrie's relatives or whomever he nominated. Now that the copyright has expired, anyone is entitled to do whatever they like with the material without paying royalties."

Craig tried to take in the concept, but before he could protest that it could not work, Eoin continued. "In this system the government gets the income, a regular income, and our country is not just used as a vehicle for rich entrepreneurs to make fat profits with little going into the coffers of Tynwald."

"But what about the art dealers, investors, people who want to put their money somewhere other than the bank, or property, or shares? What about those who gamble that their Rembrandt or their Picasso will be a good investment?"

"That's the whole point. As my friend explained it, they will still need to invest their money somewhere but they'll look for an alternative market, and so they will invest in paintings that are under a hundred years old."

"Existing artists?"

"Yes. Living artists can be taxed. Every time a picture changes hands it will be taxed. Artists will be earning and be a positive asset to the community. This way the government can fill its coffers."

There was a long silence.

"This could never happen," Craig stated.

"Governments can compulsorily purchase anything, and do," Eoin responded, unperturbed.

Craig protested, "Roads, railways, land, they purchase things like that."

"What about the right to buy?" Craig looked surprised, but Eoin hurried to explain the connection. "The right of tenant farmers to buy their farms that is being advocated by your government. It's a form of compulsory purchase, from the landowner to the tenant, sanctioned by the state."

"I still don't see how it can be done," Craig said, unconvinced.

"Tynwald," Eoin said emphatically.

"Ah! Tynwald. Of course." Craig was amused and incredulous. "You think they will pull it off?"

"If they are desperate enough, and it seems that they are, they will listen to any proposal."

"But it is ruthless!"

"Perhaps," Eoin commented abstractedly.

"On the other hand a parliament that has only in recent years abolished capital punishment, and which can still administer the birch, can obviously be ruthless."

"No one has been hanged for decades," Eoin said quietly, but Craig ignored him.

"This all has implications." Craig wasn't sure that he wanted to explore them, and was beginning to think he would prefer to join his friends in the pub.

"You and I, Craig, as dealers, might have to start looking for up and coming artists in advance of this possible law. I wouldn't want to be lumbered with unsaleable goods."

Craig stood up ready to leave. "It's not something I'm

going to have to worry about but it will be interesting to hear how it affects your island."

"Don't be too sure that it'll stop here!" Eoin joked.

Craig asked, puzzled, "Where did your contact get such an idea? It's revolutionary."

"He got it from some arty magazine he was reading, I think, said it got him thinking."

"It could only happen here!" Craig said with affection and shook Eoin's hand warmly. "Should you ever come our way, you know you're welcome."

"I know!" said Eoin, but Craig knew that they would not meet again until the next TT races.

***

For their last day on the island, John had selected the bend on the road where the expertise of the riders was most evident. Each year John and his friends purchased tickets for the Grandstand for two days, and on the other days they chose to watch from positions along the route. Although no one wanted a fatality, the fact that the TT course was so extremely dangerous contributed to its attraction, and because of this only the most skilled riders attempted it.

The crowd cheered as the last motorcycle passed on its final lap. The smell of fuel saturated the air and the haze created by the motorcycles' exhausts had not yet cleared. As the men walked along the road that had been the track a few minutes earlier they could still hear the bikes sounding like aeroplane blades as they approached, and the whine as they disappeared. Sounds were muffled and legs were stiff from standing.

"My heart was in my mouth when Aiden drove towards us; I couldn't see how he could make the bend."

"He was fantastic. Aiden's won many other races but I

bet this was his greatest achievement."

"What happened to Finch Chappell? He was in second place, but someone said he came off."

"Someone must have been injured, the medical bikes went past, did you see them?"

"Difficult to distinguish them. I think they had already passed when the marshals slowed the race."

"Finch was wearing lime and orange. I'm certain that I saw him on the fourth lap."

"You can't be sure. With bikes passing at one a second, or closer, they are still going at one hundred and thirty around this bend."

"Did you see the helicopter?"

"I was concentrating on seeing if Aiden was about to be overtaken. The biker behind him in green and black was lucky not to have a high-side crash when his rear wheel lost traction."

"Perhaps the helicopter was filming."

"It's unlikely that a race on these roads over six laps is going to escape with no casualties."

"The man I spoke to said that Aiden pranged on 'Dukes'. He's not injured, but his bike was damaged and it put him out of the race."

The crowd drifted in a disorderly fashion, John and his friends among them, almost as drained of adrenaline as those behind the windshields.

"That was the best site we have found yet." John grinned with pleasure.

They headed towards the town and peeled away once they reached the harbour to where the boat was moored, thankful that they would have no traffic, ferry queues or airport lounges to contend with.

Craig settled, exhausted, into the cabin with Taylor and Callum while Andrew went to join John at the wheel.

Andrew was a poor sailor and, with the rolling swell that began to rock the boat once they left the shelter of the island, he fared better on deck.

Craig enjoyed his annual reunion, especially with the addition of Taylor, whose career in insurance was in such contrast to his own. Taylor had by all accounts been a bright spark at school, considered by some a bit of a swot, but over their days on the Isle, Craig began to appreciate Taylor's quiet wit and refusal to be riled. None of them begrudged the fact that Taylor had a lucrative career, nor that he might be seen doing the crossword on the back of the newspaper while they were sinking their second pint.

"How was your antique crony?" Taylor asked.

Craig, having not thought about his conversation with Eoin in the excitement of the weekend, was jolted into recalling his extraordinary piece of gossip.

"Since Andrew's not here, I wouldn't want to compromise his job where he has to be seen not to profit from his position, see what you think of this. Eoin knows people from all over the island, and he told me that a friend of his, who is a member of their parliament, Tynwald, is going to put forward a new Bill. It's to make all paintings over a hundred years old the property of the state."

Callum and Taylor looked sceptical.

"I know," he sympathised with their silence, "the implications are enormous. In my business, if I were on the island, I would have to get shot of half my stock. Whether people would start investing in contemporary artists is anyone's guess. Eoin has sold his paintings already." He went on to relate all that Eoin had told him.

"He thinks it will happen?" Callum asked, amazed. "Think of the possible effect on our fellow artists. It could be sensational. Imagine the benefits for the college and all that young talent desperate to make a living." He turned towards Taylor. "What does your analytical mind make of all this?"

"Well, the island could sell the paintings from their national gallery. They would make a fortune. The government will have reduced insurance premiums, but the insurers, that's me, will be affected. In time galleries and people will buy contemporary art, and people who invest in art will shift to the newest work on the market. Money will be diverted to emerging contemporary painters."

Craig agreed. "But what if other parliaments copied Tynwald?"

Taylor thought for a moment. "There will be speculation in other parts of the country as to why they have done it. If others do follow Tynwald, the boom in sales will not last. The market will be flooded and prices decrease, but the price of contemporary art will increase. Living artists will become sought after and the government will gain on every transaction."

Although they drank abstemiously on both the outward and return trip, and John only drank on shore, he always put a crate of beer on board. All of them were cognisant of how treacherous the sea could be, and each one had been touched, to some extent, by the tragedy that had befallen one of the local fishing boats, the most serious sea disaster in the last decade or more.

After a while Craig said, "It seems that I should buy aggressively and divest myself of most of my present stock." Then he added, "What do you as a finance wizard assess might happen?"

"It's a gamble but probably worth doing," Taylor answered.

There was plenty to think about, but Craig wanted to enjoy his final evening. "I don't think we should say anything to anyone yet." Taylor and Callum nodded in agreement. "I'll keep in touch with Eoin and if he hears any more I'll let you know. It's sensible to be prepared. I would not want to be caught out."

"You won't," said Callum confidently.

"Tynwald puts its laws on the statute book once a year, in July, at the end of the parliamentary session. Any new law won't be enacted until next year. We should have plenty of notice, if this hair-brained idea goes ahead, to work out the implications."

Craig was delighted that Taylor was doing the thinking for him but when Andrew appeared to collect a beer and to ask if any of them were going to join him, they immediately followed him up the steps to the deck and all discussion ceased.

The evening was spectacular. The undulating sea, the aftermath of a storm in the Atlantic, was a welcome change from the choppy conditions of many of their homeward journeys. The sky was pale blue and streaked with pink-tinged clouds. Darkness would not fully arrive for more than an hour; it was less than a month until the longest day. Being on board was a privilege denied most of the other visitors to the island who would be queuing and jostling for ferries or aeroplanes, while they sailed peacefully towards the Solway and their home harbour.

For four days Craig's ears had been assaulted by the roar of engines and the screech of tyres, his eyes afflicted with dust and grit thrown up by the massive motorcycles and his blood racing with adrenalin. Now the sea spread in every direction and was a welcome antidote. This interlude, between the frenetic activity on the island and the humdrum routine on the mainland, was underscored by the gentle rumbling of the engine and the rhythmic splash of the waves on the prow. It felt timeless. Its peace seeped through his skin and it was one of the reasons that he kept returning, like an addict, to the Isle. Few people had the good fortune to experience such a contrast from one extreme to another, a combination of unique sensations which cemented their friendship every year.

When John brought the boat into its mooring site it was dark. They were due to work the following morning but were reluctant to disperse immediately. John, now relieved of his duties, was able to have a beer and they all congregated below.

"That was a great trip! Thanks John." Craig raised his beer can, and Callum, Andrew and Taylor followed suit. "To next year," John replied.

SEVEN

Andrew could think of no original introduction for the start of the academic year where the staff had gathered in the common room for the morning session of the in-service day. "Welcome back to McFarlane's." He swept his eyes across the room to include everyone present. "Gerald. Callum." He nodded to his senior staff before beginning a circuit of the room. The meeting would be easier to conduct than in previous years because there were no new members. However, he was aware that familiarity could lead to more spirited exchanges of views.

"Good holiday, Phyllis? You went to Sicily I seem to remember. Hot? Unbearably so?"

"When you return to this," Phyllis flung out an arm towards the window where a fine drizzle covered the glass with splashes resembling her beloved pointillism, "you are glad of the sun. Yes, it was hot but I'm not one for sunbathing." Andrew stifled a mental picture of Phyllis in a bathing suit. A contemporary artist of note had managed to romanticise the rotund female form to create an endearing nostalgia in her paintings, but when he envisaged his colleague, it was not quite so appealing. Quickly, he asked, "Did you find time to do some sketching?"

Andrew knew that Phyllis, where many of her fellow tutors did not, returned to her pad and pencil at the first opportunity. "Plenty, but that's likely to be the most I'll do this year."

"Tell me, what age were you when you started drawing, I mean, seriously drawing?"

"I was lucky. Both my parents drew when they were on holiday. It was natural for me to do the same. I suppose I was about ten years old."

"Did your parents encourage you to continue other than on holiday?"

Phyllis was puzzled. "No. It was back to schoolwork, music lessons and ballet classes!"

"Just sounding out my staff," Andrew explained as he moved on.

"Emily. How did you survive the kids this summer?"

Emily detached herself from her conversation with her colleague and, tucking a stray strand of hair behind her ear, smiled eagerly. She spoke rapidly. "Glad to be back at work, to be honest. When the weather's like this it's a job to know what to do with them. I think even they are looking forward to being back at school."

"It was Disney World you went to?"

Emily's eyes lit up. "Euro Disney, of course! It was a success. I think in a couple of years, before they are too old, we'll go again."

"Any of them showing signs of following in your foot-steps? Any budding artists?"

"The youngest isn't bad. The oldest, he's more into graphics, his drawings are precise and meticulous."

"Do they get any instruction at school?"

"As far as I know, just the usual thing. Art once a week. Handicrafts mostly."

"How about yourself, Emily, when you were young?"

"No. I just scribbled at home. Didn't do much serious stuff until I went to college."

Andrew suspected as much. Emily's work was pleasing but lacked the extra flair which was the unknown ingredient that lifted a piece of work to something remarkable, but she was a more than competent teacher and knew how to draw the best out of her students.

"Well, I am glad that you decided on college; we're the beneficiaries."

Andrew finally reached Gerald and gestured towards a couple of chairs. This was their first chance to catch up after the summer break, and it was an unspoken rule that no one joined them. Gerald took off his leather jacket and hung it on the back of a chair. The two men did occasionally meet in the town but their lives otherwise did not overlap. Gerald, being a relative newcomer, had his own circle of friends and was not part of Andrew's tightly knit group who had been born and bred in the area. At work this difference was healthy and Andrew's policy, although stimulated by Gerald's ideas, was to keep him on side since he was the member of staff most likely to raise objections.

"Good break, Gerald?"

"Yes, you?"

"You'll be pleased with the degree results," Andrew said.

"Delighted. We must be doing something right. What's the intake like this year?"

"Much the same but I must say I'd like to see an increase in applications. That would secure future years but I want to see a continued upward movement in the quality of our new students. If we had a larger base to choose from, this would help."

"It's a difficult one," Gerald admitted. "We're still an infant establishment, we have no past students who are able to spread the word, nor have we had time to produce any artists who have made a name for themselves that we can boast about, and we can't rely solely on your Abigail."

Andrew, anticipating Gerald's reference to Jacob's daughter and remembering his antagonism because she might be treated as a special case, said, "We made no exceptions for that girl, she's talented, but you're right, we need students from further afield."

He moved on quickly to deflect from the subject. "Gerald, perhaps we need a different way of attracting students; after all we don't have to follow the same rules as other colleges. Churning out the same curriculum as other colleges while they have years of credentials behind them, isn't going to work. The problem is that we can't predict which students are going to shine by their final year and we need a way of judging their development before they come here."

"So you are saying that we need more students and a better way of judging their quality? Don't the school folios give you some idea?"

"Their folios are a snapshot of where they are now. We have no way of seeing whether they are on an upward curve. Compare them to students who take music exams. The music colleges are equipped to judge because their students have had to complete grade after grade, and during this process the dross drops out. We have nothing like that. Think about it for me!"

Andrew collected a cup of coffee from the machine wishing he could have avoided it in favour of the filter coffee in his office, but holding a mug was somehow a necessary accessory to opening the meeting. Andrew wandered across to the centre of the room, stirring his coffee. Talking ceased while the staff settled back into armchairs.

Faces looked up and Gerald saw the effect of Andrew's enviable charisma. "He could ask them to work through the summer and they would do it for him," he thought.

From his briefcase Andrew extracted some papers and handed them out. Gerald listened with his usual measure of scepticism as Andrew began to speak.

"I won't recap all the achievements of McFarlane's College since its inception, but I will highlight a few of the innovations that have distinguished it from other colleges." Gerald was familiar with the catalogue. "We have individual studios for our final-year students which are shared with working artists, some from far afield. We have a vigorous Friends society which promotes our shows, and some sponsorships thanks to our benefactor after whom the college is named. Finally, but most importantly, we have our highly dedicated and talented staff."

Andrew swept his gaze around the captivated faces of his staff. He was acutely aware of their loyalty to him, even Gerald's.

"I'll go over the points in turn and then we'll break for discussion. As you can see we've had some directives from Education this year. First, our funding is tied in with evidence of our commitment to engaging with the community. Second, we need to produce innovative ideas that will promote McFarlane's. Third, we need to show that we can compete on equal terms with other colleges in attracting students."

Andrew continued to read out the items but became distracted by Gerald's change in attitude. Holding his agenda to one side, Gerald was sitting forward and staring, obviously disgruntled.

As he came to the last point on the agenda, Andrew took the opportunity to gauge the reactions of the rest of his staff, but saw nothing that might indicate that they were upset.

"Any questions?" Andrew kept his gaze away from Gerald. "Everyone all right so far?" There was a consensus of agreement until he pressed them. "Anything from last year that you feel we should change? I'm not on the shop floor, remember!"

"Just one thing," one of the group responded. "I would like some contact with the final-year students. It's one thing to help their development, but it would be good to have some input with the final product." A few heads nodded.

Andrew smiled thoughtfully. "I understand, but the students might be confused by too much advice, especially having gained a lot from you in their first and second years." He was rewarded with a smile from Emily. "I have a project in mind that might satisfy this request." He looked around from face to face and said enigmatically, "What is coming up later today might interest you."

Gerald held up the agenda and faces turned towards him. "Andrew." He pointed to the sheet of paper and stabbed at it as he spoke. "Do you not think it would have made a more sensible discussion if some of us, if not all of us, had been sent this in advance? These are major changes. The senior staff at least could have been notified."

"I see your point, Gerald." He searched for Callum and Emily's reactions. They seemed to find this as unexpected as he did. "Indeed, I thought it over, but the new directives involve everyone and there was no chance to circulate them."

"We're meant to discuss and make decisions today?"

Andrew felt the tension reaching all the members of the staff room. "This afternoon's workshop is set aside for brainstorming. I need everyone's input and I suggest that we have another meeting, say, in two days' time. That will give you time to form your own opinions. We'll consider all aspects then."

Gerald appeared to be only partly mollified. "Let's break for lunch." The room cleared quickly but Andrew held back, knowing that Gerald would have more to say.

"Andrew, I'm your deputy, I'm not sure that springing

this on us at this meeting was the best idea."

"Gerald, believe me, I only received this a few days ago. Officially the term starts today. You are more likely than any of the others to come up with practical strategies, but I have to bring them on board. For the sake of the college give these your attention and help me plan."

Andrew noticed that Gerald's demeanour relaxed slightly. "All right. I'll do it. Be prepared for some radical solutions and I'll discuss them with you before the next meeting."

"Before," Andrew repeated.

Gerald gave a short nod. "Agreed."

At the end of the day Callum watched Gerald leave with a group of tutors around him. He conjectured that they were heading for the King's Arms where they would no doubt thrash out the developments to the curriculum that Andrew had outlined. It would be a lively and heated debate, something that Callum avoided, but he wondered whether Gerald would wholeheartedly support Andrew.

Callum saw advantages in all of Andrew's changes. There was a need to encourage more students to apply, ensuring that they stayed the course and were genuinely keen and dedicated. He was interested in the idea that they could provide a form of qualification which when they left the college enabled them to run their own art courses without undertaking a year of teacher training. In particular Andrew seemed to be aware of the frustrations of the junior tutors and felt that there was little that Gerald could object to.

"Callum! Just a minute!" Andrew caught up with him. "Are you in a hurry?"

Andrew and Callum had not only grown up together but they had kept in touch despite their paths diverging for a number of years. Callum did not find teaching large groups easy, and his timetable for some time had reflected this. He wondered whether his friend was now having to make changes.

"This new requirement from the council where we need to show that we have an outreach programme. It's to placate the tax payers. What do you think?"

Callum stalled. "It sounds like a major commitment."

"The new directive, which has been issued to all the colleges, might prove to be to your advantage and I wanted to sound you out before suggesting any innovations to the curriculum. There's one aspect that could be awkward unless we approach it cautiously and that's the role that I think you should fill. The thing is, I was wondering if you would head it up. It would be mostly administration." As Callum weighed up the implications, Andrew added, "I think in the first instance we should keep the project small."

Callum gave a sigh of relief. "So what have you got in mind?"

"I was thinking that you might supervise the diploma project for the final-year students and create a rota for some of the junior tutors who would like to be involved. There's quite a lot of detail yet to sort out, but I'd like it if you would consider the role. It would mean a reduction in your teaching hours."

"I can't resist this. Do you really think that I am best suited for it?"

Callum wondered how Gerald would take to this news. It might be that Gerald would consider, as deputy, that he should be given the job, or at least offered it. However, Andrew had a way of achieving the outcomes that he wanted, and as this coincided with a change for the better for himself, Callum decided to ignore his misgivings. Besides, he thought that Andrew's idea of awarding a teaching diploma was inspired and after a few moments he added, "Andrew, I am certain that no other college will be creating a teaching diploma. Where did you get the idea?"

"Oh! My wife. She was at the dentist's and picked up a glossy. I think it's called *Inside and Out*. She came home inspired by an article she had read."

"Well, tell her she's solved one of our problems."

Andrew looked pleased. "I told her to look out for some more ideas next time she has her teeth looked at."

EIGHT

The centre of the town was dominated by a church and the ruins of a castle surrounded by a substantial area of grass, triangular in shape. A tourist could either turn right towards the harbour and follow the road around to the castle or continue onwards along the main street past the church.

Opposite the church, among a row of gift shops, was an art gallery. The exterior had been newly painted so that it was the first to catch the eye. Gerald stood on the pavement and surveyed his handiwork, which he had completed in the early weeks of the summer before the majority of the tourists arrived. The lettering had been beyond his capabilities and he had employed a local sign writer. The effect was pleasing and the restrained colouring did not detract from the display windows. These were large and required some skill in window dressing but Gerald was happy to credit his wife Kerry with quite a flair. She was self-taught and possessed a good eye. She had a gift, too, for securing a sale. Gerald had learnt to refrain from giving his opinion on her purchases because, although he was often confounded by her choices, the success of her business had often proved her correct. He and Kerry had eventually come to the conclusion that art at college and commercial art needed different mindsets.

Gerald was keen to discuss Andrew's plans for the college but he knew that he would probably have to wait until Kerry closed the shop. He entered quietly. Kerry was engaged with a customer and while he waited he noticed that there was some new stock on display. He appreciated the ceramic bowls and pottery figures but he had an immediate and instinctive dislike of her choice of paintings. Finally the door closed behind the customers.

"I can't believe these are going to sell." Despite their agreement to refrain from interfering in each other's sphere of work, Gerald could not resist baiting her at times. He pointed to a collection of miniature paintings in garish colours with old-gold frames. "I know you'll prove me wrong, but where would you put these if they were yours?"

Kerry looked up from her desk and grinned. "You'll be surprised, but dark paint, heavy old-fashioned curtains and mahogany are the rage. These complement the décor."

"How do you know? It beats me." Gerald went across the room, skirted a display table, and joined Kerry behind the desk. After a while, glancing up from her computer, Kerry asked, "How was your first day back?"

"Apart from the fact that Andrew is crowing because Jacob's daughter is one of the new students?"

"Oh, Gerald, let it go. Tell me what was discussed at the meeting."

The door opened and a family entered. Their eyes averted, the two teenage girls were awkward, and their parents were only slightly less so.

Kerry swung her chair towards Gerald to whisper, "Passing the time!" before standing to greet them. She then sorted some papers on her desk while her customers browsed. When they left she asked him, "Do you think that I would be allowed to hang some of your students' work?"

Gerald was surprised. Kerry had not previously shown more than a passing interest in the work of his students, although she always attended the degree show. "Why not? I have been thinking for a while that the students needed an outlet, but I hesitated ever to ask you; after all it's your shop and not a charity for aspiring artists. I think it is a great idea. Where did that one come from?"

"My magazine! I read an article where it seems that the emphasis will be on unknown artists and I want to be part of it."

Gerald was sceptical but delighted that one of the plans that he had been concocting since Andrew's talk was being suggested by Kerry unprompted. It would involve an increase in his workload, but it might help Kerry and for that reason alone it was worth it.

Another group entered the shop and Gerald said quietly, "I'll push off. Do they look more hopeful?"

Kerry smiled encouragingly at the newcomers before answering him. "I'll tell you later. A coffee would be good."

It was unfortunate that when Kerry was at her most stretched, Gerald had time on his hands. Kerry used to ask him why he did not paint during the long summer holidays but she had no experience of the practical side of being an artist and Gerald explained that after the rigours of the academic year he had not the energy to make the required effort. He said that he had deferred creating his own art until he retired, when he resolved to restart. Kerry said that she hoped this wasn't wishful thinking.

"Here you are." Gerald handed Kerry her coffee in one of their oldest mugs. Kerry made a face.

"Gerald. I am here to project a certain image. One of our Wright mugs which are elegant and fun is more in keeping with people's impression of a gallery owner. If you sell attractive objects it seems perverse then to be seen using a faded mug bought from some souvenir shop."

Gerald decided to ignore her and lifted his hands in an exaggerated gesture.

It was an hour later that Kerry joined Gerald in the kitchen. She closed and locked the door to the shop which connected to their house. The property was spacious with a long, narrow garden that provided privacy and peace and the house not only extended into a sun-room but Kerry had designed a first-floor living room which gave them a view towards the harbour and the hills beyond the estuary.

Although Gerald was eager to discuss his day at the college, he was anxious not to overwhelm her immediately with his account and the plans that he was formulating as a result of Andrew's proposed programme. He continued his earlier conversation.

"So where do you find out about the current trends? How, now that we are tucked away in this rural idyll, are you able to gauge people's tastes?"

"Fashion magazines, I'm afraid," Kerry answered as she perched beside the counter to watch Gerald prepare their meal. "A waste of money for some, perhaps, but it's my way of keeping a finger on the pulse."

When they finished their meal Gerald refilled their glasses. "Shall we take these upstairs?"

Kerry asked as she followed him, "Have you something on your mind?"

Although autumn was approaching, some light remained in the sky and the warmth of the sun lingered in the room. Gerald settled into one of the armchairs and gazed vacantly out of the window, silently reviewing the day's discussion.

He had been impressed by Andrew's proposals, although if he was honest he had felt side-lined. This undoubtedly had been the impetus that had spurred him into developing his own scheme, one that would meet with the year's aim and Andrew's vision, but which would also enhance his own profile. He had always been concerned by the fact that students graduated from college without a qualification to teach, but Andrew had pre-empted him, and knowing that he was now open to ideas, Gerald was hopeful that his own ambitious plan might be adopted.

"It's like this. Andrew has asked us to come up with ideas for this year which engage the college with the community. It's to satisfy the requirements of the local authority. Andrew seems to have some plans in place already."

"What are they?"

"It's far-sighted, I must give him that. If we could award a teaching diploma or certificate to the students once they complete a course working with schoolchildren, it would be helpful for the students once they graduate. It would give them credibility if they had tangible recognition in the form of a qualification. He is planning to run art classes as an after-school activity, and the final-year students will do the teaching. Some of the junior staff have been angling to have input with that group and so he has cleverly inveigled them into supervising. I suspect that Callum will be in charge, which will suit him, and allow him to reduce his teaching hours."

"Andrew has untold depths of subterfuge." Kerry smiled. "You mean that they would have a qualification allowing them to give lessons and take evening classes?"

"Even better than that, although it is an important part of it, we would begin to see art classes developing in the community. Andrew quite rightly says that exams and folios show us so little, whereas if we could assess a student's work over time we would have a better idea of their development and potential."

"I see," Kerry said.

"Also you can assess if they are dedicated and prepared to stick out a whole course."

"If that is Andrew's project for Callum, what is yours?" Kerry asked. "How are you going to upstage Callum?"

Gerald shifted in his chair, holding his glass while swirling the remains of the wine. "Each year should have a show and not limit it to the final year. We have the space, but only for one show at a time. I've thought about it and we could manage one at the end of each term and not restrict it to once a year in the summer." He paused before enlarging on the logistics. "The first years would show at the end of the Easter term, and the second years at Christmas and the final show would remain as usual in May and June."

"That might work," Kerry said encouragingly. "It would give each year time to amass enough material. Your first- and second-year students would feel that everything they produce has the potential to be an exhibit. At the onset of the course it must appear to the new students that the work they produce does not matter because it is such a long time until the degree show. I think you should put the idea to Andrew."

It was nearly dark outside but neither moved to switch on the lights. Their eyes grew accustomed to the gloom and they never tired of the scene. No matter what the weather, the view across the estuary to the hills was arresting, and every change of season showed a different aspect of the countryside. It did not take an artist to appreciate the nuances of cloud or sunset, snow or sunshine.

Gerald followed his train of thought. "So long as I don't have to mount each show!"

"Gerald, no one but I know the work that you put into the summer one." Kerry moved across to sit beside Gerald and rested her head on his shoulder. "I also realise that you get frustrated with the college and want to drive it forward faster and establish it as a leader in providing courses for student artists. Perhaps now is your opportunity."

"That is my aim."

"Andrew would probably be content for you to run that project, which I know is what you want. What is more, you can delegate responsibility to the junior tutors."

Gerald appreciated her echoing Andrew's solution to the reorganisation of staff duties. He thought for a moment and then chuckled. "You wanted to try hanging some students' paintings in the shop. Now you'll have regular opportunities to scout out talented young artists."

"That thought had entered my mind," laughed Kerry, "I'm sure it won't be the paramount reason, but I am always on the look-out for talent, and, to be fair, it would be to our mutual advantage."

"I might use it as a selling point to Andrew. It's an outlet to the community." He placed an arm around her shoulders. Kerry felt relaxed and her presence had a similar effect on him. He chose his words carefully. "Kerry, you are a master at extracting the best from a situation. I am confident that this germ of an enterprise is ready to be launched."

Gerald picked up a glossy magazine from the coffee table and was soon immersed; the ideas that he had tested out with Kerry were now safely endorsed by her and his minor irritation with Andrew dispelled.

NINE

The spring term at McFarlane's College was well under way, the tutors and students were settled into a routine and teething troubles resolved. Gerald was supervising his Thursday afternoon class when Andrew wandered in. The sounds of squeaking easels, rattling paint tins and running water as paintbrushes were cleaned or water pots filled, ceased abruptly. Andrew was always amused at the effect of his entry on a group of students. They appeared to anticipate that he might circulate and dispense his critical appraisal, despite the fact that this was a function he rarely performed. However, on this occasion Gerald, who was standing with a student discussing his painting, moved back from the easel and invited Andrew to join them.

"Your opinion, Andrew?" It was immediately apparent why Gerald had misgivings about the student's work and Andrew was not surprised that his help had been solicited.

The young student looked apprehensively from face to face. Andrew took his time as he studied the young man's work and then chose his words carefully.

"What do you think? Do you know where you are going with this?"

"Not really. I thought I did, but the more I worked on it, the more confused I became."

Andrew paused before he answered. "You have an interesting idea. Can you figure out another method of expressing it?"

"I'm not sure. I should probably start again," the student said doubtfully.

"That's probably your best plan. Think about your aim and then let rip. You've done it before!"

The student looked earnestly at Andrew, lifted his canvas from the easel and rewarded both men with a shy smile.

Andrew drew Gerald to one side and led the way through the door into the corridor. "I haven't really come here to take over your class."

"I didn't think so!" Gerald replied.

"Can they spare you? I'd like a bit of your time and advice."

"An hour if you like, they are working well."

"An hour would be ideal."

Gerald informed his class that he was called away and followed Andrew, who proceeded to stride down the corridor to the rear exit. As they turned to walk down the lane towards the harbour Andrew said, "We are heading for the warehouse."

"The one that was bought and partially renovated?"

"That's the one. I want to introduce you to Taylor. He's bought the building to create a site for exhibitions. Since this town, because of its associations with Oppenheimer, Jessie King and Hornel, has recently been named The Artist's Town, Taylor thought he would cash in on it! I am being a bit unfair but it's a good opportunity as an investment, and the choice of this town was logical."

This was not strictly true. Andrew suspected that Taylor's decision to relocate and start up a new venture was a deliberate attempt to remove himself from all that reminded him of his shared life before he was widowed. It had been a generous gesture by John to invite him to the Isle of Man and the camaraderie forged over that time must have been a factor in reshaping his future alone.

While he admired Taylor's attitude to risk and appreciated that he was in a position to take a financial hit, Andrew saw no reason why he should not also, on behalf of his college and therefore his own position as principal, take advantage of this enterprise. He was certain that Gerald would not be slow to realise its potential since their ambitions for the college were an area in which they fundamentally agreed.

They walked the short distance from the college to the harbour, passing a few stone cottages that had not yet been turned into picture-book idylls, until they came to the warehouse where the main door was already open.

***

The warehouse was worthy of being preserved. Built into the wall of the harbour and serving fishermen for decades, the stone building, abandoned for some time, had been an integral part of the industry. Renovated by a speculator, the roof and stonework were intact, but then money was a problem and no one seemed to find a commercial use for it. In the centre of the empty shell of the warehouse, Taylor was studying plans on a large sheet of paper held by a younger man. He hurried across the vast building to greet Andrew.

Taylor was dressed in a three-piece suit and the contrast with Gerald's leather jacket, open neck shirt and suede shoes was stark. Although Gerald was audacious when in his role as a teacher, Andrew was aware that in an unfamiliar setting his usual bravado was checked.

"Good of you to come over so quickly," Taylor said enthusiastically.

They shook hands and Andrew introduced Gerald. "My senior tutor." He was relieved to see that Taylor accorded

him the same attention. "Excellent! Ah! Martin, my architect."

Martin spread out the large sheet of drawings so that
Andrew and Gerald could study them. The neatness
and precision of the architect's design was a relief from
the abstract slashes of paint currently being produced
by Gerald's class. Martin leant over to point out various
features. "If the building is used as an exhibition hall for
paintings, then you will probably find that it will adapt for
many other occasions."

"Any occasion, but not weddings!" Taylor added from
behind, sounding appalled at the idea.

"The kitchen and toilets will be too small for large-scale
catering," Martin reassured him. "A serviceable kitchen for
drinks and light finger foods, and stylish toilets are all you
need. I suspect that there won't be a demand for more. The
exterior of the building and the roof are water-tight, we'll
replace the windows and level the floor. The outer walls
are in good condition, and the building will soon be ready
for installation of inner walls, plumbing and electricity."

"This seems already in an advanced stage and near com-
pletion. Are you asking us for our opinions?" Gerald asked
abruptly.

"The details for the interior have yet to be designed,"
Martin answered in a measured tone. "Are there any
pitfalls we need to avoid when it comes to mounting art
shows?" Martin included all three men with his question.

Gerald pointed to an end wall. "There is rarely sufficient
wall space for large pictures. That end wall should be
kept so that we could use its full length. Paintings are not
shown to advantage if they are cramped on a wall with a
low ceiling. I take it that you are having two levels?" He
bent over to indicate to Martin what he envisaged.

Taylor gave Andrew a quizzical look. Andrew responded

with the slightest nod of his head to assure Taylor that he should take the suggestion.

Martin took out a pad and pencil and drew a sketch. "Something like this? A spiral staircase and only half of the building with an upper floor?" Andrew noticed that Gerald kept silent, no doubt feeling that his contribution constituted a minor victory.

"Lighting is important," Andrew emphasised. "It contributes to an exhibition almost to the exclusion of everything else. How much natural light can you put into the design?"

Martin was eager to explain. "The windows can all have blinds. Lighting will be flexible. In winter you will need artificial light and I can incorporate bulbs fixed on wires that can be placed anywhere. You'll have seen them in more modern galleries."

Gerald turned to Andrew and his endorsement of the project was clear. "I can see many future possibilities for your building. If we could rent it for our shows, it would free up studio space and give events a higher profile." He hesitated. "If we could afford it!" he added, glancing at Andrew, but Taylor was quick to intervene.

"I've thought this out. So long as I cover running costs I can afford to think of the building as an investment."

Martin paced out the area he calculated would be needed for the kitchen, toilets and storeroom, and described how he envisaged the smaller room under the split level. "The staircase would be here in the centre. The entrance hall would be roomy to allow for a desk and a hallway with enough room for people to remove their coats, and park their umbrellas." Martin smiled, and his concession to the reputation of the Scottish weather was not lost on the group.

Martin wrote a few notes on his pad. "I'm afraid that I

have another appointment. I will be in touch!"

"What do you think? Anything to add?" Taylor asked, once his architect had left.

Gerald answered, "So what is the grand opening to be?"

"We've spoken about that." Andrew turned towards Taylor. "We decided that an exhibition by a local artist would send the right message. We've invited Jacob."

"The mysterious and enigmatic Jacob?"

"You don't know him?" Taylor asked.

"Only by reputation. Has he agreed?" Gerald asked incredulously.

"He will confirm his commitment once he's seen this place." Andrew looked at his watch. "He should be here in a few minutes."

When Jacob arrived he looked exactly as Gerald had imagined. Wearing an ancient leather waistcoat, a tidy shirt and presentable cord trousers, he had the face of a biblical prophet. Thick unruly hair grew erratically above a broad forehead and his beard covered half his face. His skin was weather-beaten, which was to be expected from his outdoor lifestyle and, combined with his tall stature, he unconsciously dominated the space. Gerald had not bargained for the physical presence of the artist. He had no preconception of Jacob through his paintings and therefore his first impression was gained by absorbing his aura of self-confidence, one which exuded neither arrogance nor condescension. Gerald warmed to him at once. When he was introduced, Jacob's handshake was unexpectedly gentle.

Taylor escorted Jacob around the building and explained the layout. He appeared to visualise clearly the completed building and on hearing the description of the large wall space at one end of the room he beamed. His voice was deep and melodious.

"That will be grand! Was that your idea?"

"It was Gerald's, all the credit goes to him."

Gerald felt unexpectedly flattered that his suggestion was received with such enthusiasm.

"How many pictures do you think?" Jacob asked.

"You'll exhibit at the opening then?" Andrew's excitement was undisguised. Gerald already felt that Jacob was a good choice, if only for the strength of his personality.

"I would be honoured," Jacob replied.

Taylor stretched out his arms in an expansive gesture. "In which case we would leave the choice up to you. I understand that some of your canvasses are nearly six foot in height, and you would not want to crowd the walls. On the other hand, there is ample space for a good twenty or twenty-five, I would say."

Jacob spent a few moments calculating space. "About twenty paintings, I should imagine."

"I'll insure them for you," Taylor offered.

Jacob gave a chuckle. "Nothing of mine has ever been insured."

"Well you had better start now. I'll do it," Taylor insisted.

Jacob turned to Andrew. "What will you do with the smaller place? I won't be able to use that."

"We wondered about asking your wife, Deborah?" Andrew ventured. Gerald watched Jacob's reaction. It was one of pure delight with no artifice. He did not need to answer.

TEN

"We're worried about Abi," Reuben said as Tansy pressed her foot on the accelerator to join the motorway, and settled the car into the inside lane.

"What's happened? She seemed fine at New Year."

"That's what I thought but I suppose we have both been preoccupied with our jobs. How's yours going?"

"The last few weeks have been hectic. So much of what I cover happens at weekends. I'm sorry I haven't been free before now to come to your parents' house. The job is going well, my editor is pleased, apparently, with my refreshing style and my reliability." Tansy glanced quickly away from the wheel to see if Reuben was amused. As he still seemed perturbed she said, "But tell me about Abi."

"I don't know as much as I should, we don't communicate regularly. Like you I've been rather engrossed in work. It's pretty grim, the work itself, shackled for hours to columns of figures displayed on identical screens, but when we get together after work it's as if the collective energy from so many young people explodes."

"Will you stick it?"

"If some degree of problem solving is introduced before long the work will be less tedious and more of a challenge. To date there's been no such distraction. However, as we learnt at school, you have to endure some uninteresting subjects if you want to get to university and I expected these initial months to be a grind. If I want a permanent job it is probably a rite of passage."

Many of their friends had moved away or were embracing comfortable domesticity, but Reuben and Tansy both felt they were only on the first steps of their respective careers. Tansy glanced at her rear view mirror before changing lanes and negotiated the roundabout which marked the end of the motorway. She was aware of Reuben's dissatisfaction and refrained from expressing the exhilaration that she derived from her writing; wanting to recapture the carefree times of their student years, she spoke very little about her work. Once they were on the country roads she returned to their earlier conversation.

"How did you hear about Abi?"

"Florrie. She wrote that Abi has got thin and that she leaves early and always takes the last bus home."

"There must be something else. That on its own isn't enough to worry about."

"Florrie says that she's evasive and never volunteers anything. She used to have an opinion on every subject."

***

Reuben had arranged for them to meet up with David and Abigail that evening, but when they reached the pub David was alone. They had not been certain that David would be able to join them because of the erratic hours kept by the fishing boats, but he had been enthusiastic and implied that Abigail would be with him. He looked uncharacteristically tidy, his hair recently cut and wearing a casual jacket and tailored trousers instead of his habitual sweatshirt and jeans. This gave him an air of responsibility as if he had aged since they had last seen him.

"Abi's shift at the Harbour Café doesn't finish until ten thirty. She told me she had changed it but then an hour ago she rang to say that the other girl hadn't turned up."

"They must sell a lot of fish and chips," Tansy said flippantly, but she suddenly saw David's dejected face and realised that her remark was inappropriate. "Sorry!"

"I don't think she's telling me the truth," David said in a flat voice.

Tansy could feel Reuben's reaction and feared that he would leap to his sister's defence before David had time to finish. She placed a restraining hand on his arm.

David suddenly looked haggard. "I don't mean she's lying exactly. I just feel that she is avoiding talking to me."

"That seems unlike Abi," Reuben said, "except that Florrie told us she's become monosyllabic at home."

Tansy shifted in her chair. She hoped that David would confide in them and tell them what he suspected were the reasons for Abigail's behaviour but was unsure whether he would want to include her. Wondering if she should leave, she glanced at Reuben but when he said nothing to indicate that David wished to speak to him alone, she asked gently, "David, what's happening?"

David did not answer immediately, then he leaned forward and seemed to come to a decision. "I might as well tell you, or you might jump to the wrong conclusions and imagine something really bad, like drugs."

Reuben shot back in his seat. "Drugs? Abi wouldn't take drugs, she was vocal about it at school. None of us are interested. I've been offered them and I expect she has too but, if it's not drugs, then what?"

"I have left the boats, I am no longer working for my Dad, I have taken a shore job." David avoided his question and Reuben knew not to press him.

"When was this? Florrie never said anything about you working on shore. Well, of course she wouldn't know about it because Abi's not been communicating."

"About a month ago the weather was too bad for us to go to sea, so I went to meet Abi after college but she never turned up. I asked a few people in the town and eventually I discovered that she was waitressing at the Harbour Café, across from the car park. She wouldn't say anything, or apologise, so I asked when she was due to finish. She told me 'in time to get the bus'. I knew it left at nine thirty and decided to catch her as she walked to the bus stop. She wouldn't talk, just looked at the ground. I asked her if it was anything that I had done. I stood with her until the bus arrived and then she said, 'I promise it's not you.' But things got worse. For a few nights I walked her to the bus, but I had the same reaction each time. This was doing my nut, so eventually I decided to go into college and find out the time of her lunch break. The receptionist said that she wasn't in."

"But Florrie said she left every morning," Reuben said, puzzled. "If things have got worse is it because she is upset about the exhibition?"

"What exhibition is that? Abi hasn't got a show this term, has she?" David looked to Tansy for an explanation.

"Didn't you know? There's a new gallery opening by the harbour and Jacob is exhibiting for their inaugural show."

"Why would that upset Abi?" This time he turned to Reuben.

Tansy was curious. "Surely you are excited that Jacob has this opportunity?" She too looked towards Reuben.

They had to wait for his response. "What if no one likes his paintings? What if people misunderstand them or ridicule them?"

"Why should they?" Tansy persisted.

"That's what happens, and Abi will be in the centre of it all, especially afterwards at college."

"Now I see your point," David said. "Do you think that Abi feels responsible for its success?"

"She will," Reuben said urgently, "and so will I. I've felt this before, at the last exhibition, when hardly any pictures were sold and I know how Abi feels. Although it is only an exhibition and no sales are expected, if the general reaction is unfriendly she's the one who will feel humiliated."

"And Jacob?" Tansy ventured.

"No one knows." Reuben was still on edge. "But I know why Abi isn't at college now. It's the pressure. It'll put her off so much that she won't dare go back."

"That explains everything, Reuben. Abi is working. She works all day." David gave a sigh. "It was getting hard to talk to her. Yesterday I went early to the bus stop. Oh, Tansy. When she arrived in town she looked awful and when she saw me she looked scared. I told her that I did not care if she was late for work because she was going nowhere until I found out what was going on. It was cold and none of the cafés were open so I said that we would walk all the way to Beatties, the bakers by the post office. That's when she started to cry."

Tansy and Reuben did not attempt to interrupt, and David seemed eager to unburden himself.

"She can't draw. She was crying so hard that was all I heard at first. She can't paint. She felt that everyone was watching her, that she was somehow different and she should be producing the best work. I held her for ages and when she was calm we went into the bakery and found a corner table. She has not found anyone she likes on the course and she thinks that every comment made by the tutors is a criticism."

"That's quite possible," Tansy observed. "She must have absorbed so much from her parents."

Reuben looked surprised. "I had not thought of that. Go on."

"So she spent more and more time in the other departments, like animation and ceramics, and then became embarrassed to go in at all. She's lost all confidence. That's when I told my Dad that I couldn't go out on the boats for a while."

"What did he say? Wasn't he angry?" Reuben asked.

"I thought he would be but he seemed to understand. So I've found a job with Lauren McGill, the MSP. She was advertising a position in her office. As it's computer work, answering the telephone and being nice to people, it's a job I can do."

"Why did you have to change your job?"

"Abi was wearing herself out, working all the time, pretending to be at college and never taking a break. Now, I can at least get her to come back to our house in the evenings. She made me promise not to tell your parents. Luckily she didn't make me promise not to tell you," David ended with a weak smile.

"What about her grant? She has to attend," Tansy said.

"That's what I told her. She could just register and then disappear but she says she's earning enough and not to worry."

Tansy was unconvinced. "Won't Jacob and Deborah find out when they start to organise the exhibition?"

"Tutors aren't allowed to divulge information about their students but I can't imagine what they think. I wish she'd tell them."

"We may be able to persuade her, but what is she going to do? She can't hide like this for ever," Reuben objected. "I could tackle her head on."

"But I've been trying for weeks, using every tactic I can think of. I've suggested changing colleges, or admitting it is a mistake, but she won't do either."

Although she might be judged as interfering if she attempted to mediate, Tansy felt that she should offer. "Could I help, since I'm neither family nor from the college?" She worried that David was shouldering the whole burden.

Reuben gave her a grateful look. "Let's wait until Abi arrives and take it from there. You can't sort this out on your own, David."

Their conversation turned to other subjects and finally Abigail appeared. Tansy was distressed at the change in her. Her skin was pasty white and unhealthy with spots poorly disguised by heavy makeup. Her eyes, unnaturally bright as if she was withholding tears, were outlined with a dark mascara which augmented their prominence. Her once luxuriously abundant brown hair was now lank and scraped back off her face with a tight scrunchie, and yet, despite these physical changes, it was Abigail's air of disengagement that troubled her the most.

They were all silent as Abigail made her way towards them. She seemed mildly surprised to see her brother and Tansy, as if she had forgotten their arrangement, but she did not attempt to leave. She sat down close to David and took his hand. "I suppose you know," she said.

ELEVEN

Jacob and Deborah were the only two people who looked out of place at their exhibition. Jacob wore the battered leather jacket and cord trousers that he had worn on his previous visit to the building, and Deborah looked quaint and old-fashioned in a floral blouse and mid-calf skirt.

Taylor, dressed in a grey-blue suit with matching tie, stood by the entrance to welcome everyone. He had laid on wine and canapés, employing a local company to supply and serve the refreshments. He had consulted with Andrew and compiled an impressive list of guests representing large and small local businesses, councillors, teachers from the nearby secondary schools, and their MSP Lauren McGill. Andrew had also suggested inviting the final-year students and as a result the whole of the lower floor was crowded, a gradual crescendo of noise filling the building.

Andrew circulated, keen to create a good impression for the college. He was disappointed that Craig, as the only art dealer invited, had not appeared and he also noticed that Abigail was not with her family.

"Gerald." Andrew beckoned to him and Gerald threaded his way through the crowd followed by his wife. "You've met Jacob, but let me introduce Deborah. Gerald. Kerry."

Kerry was quite at ease at functions such as these where she had to meet new people and quickly strike up a rapport. "This is a thrilling day for the town, and I'm delighted to meet you both." She directed the conversation towards

Deborah. "I've had a chance to look at your paintings. It is like discovering a hidden gem." Deborah looked pleased but still remained silent until Kerry explained that she owned a gallery and then Deborah said, "I have passed your shop, and admired your window."

"Come in next time. Tuesdays are usually quiet. We could talk." Kerry was inwardly amused that Deborah seemed surprised and even somewhat alarmed by this invitation.

Meanwhile Gerald asked Jacob if they could go up the stairs and see the paintings on the end wall in relative peace. Gerald had not seen any of Jacob's work and he was affected more than he had been for some years by the power of the paintings. Jacob was relieved to be taken away from the melee and to have a chance to discuss art with another artist.

"Your work, Gerald, do you have time?"

Gerald shrugged. "I'm increasingly aware that I have more to give as a teacher than by pursuing my own painting. I think there comes a moment when you accept the limits of your talent. No amount of hard work is going to change that, but I gain satisfaction from enabling the next generation to reach their potential."

"That's a particularly admirable goal," Jacob said appreciatively. Their private interlude did not last long as other guests drifted towards the upper level, where, for those who wanted to speak to him, Jacob was more accessible.

When Andrew was reassured that Jacob and Deborah no longer needed chaperoning, he turned his attention to his second task. It was imperative that the councillors were convinced of the necessity of supporting his college. He gathered an entourage of councillors around him, they tended to clump together, and explained to them how he had implemented his outreach programme and how beneficial it had been to his students. Andrew knew how to flatter and credit them with more than they deserved, and he reckoned that he had hit the mark.

Tansy waited with Reuben and his sisters until the number of guests arriving through the door dwindled.

"Do you think this is a good moment to speak to Taylor?" she asked Reuben.

"Do you want me to come over with you?"

"Stay with the girls. You'll recognise a few people. I know no one."

Tansy had dressed carefully for the occasion, hoping that Taylor would be impressed by her professionalism. When she looked around she realised that there weren't many women of her age in the crowd and as she approached Taylor she was pleased that he remembered her. "You're with Jacob." He greeted her.

"Reuben told me to introduce myself."

Taylor, ignoring all other demands on him as a host, focused his attention on Tansy. "What can I do for you?"

"I'm Tansy. I'm a journalist for *Inside and Out*." Taylor looked perplexed. "It's a monthly magazine featuring town houses and gardens. I write an article on art. I thought, if you don't mind, I would interview a few people?"

"Can I show you around? Or introduce you to anyone?" Taylor led her to the centre of the room.

"You'll be occupied and Reuben can help me. But I was wondering if you would answer a couple of questions?"

"You want to start by interviewing me?"

"If you don't mind."

"I always thought that it was other people who gave interviews, spokesmen, you know!" Taylor took a moment to survey the scene. They looked across at the throngs of people holding drinks and talking to each other.

"My slant is why art is important in a community. Is it important?"

They were almost the same height and Taylor responded to her earnest manner and respectful diffidence with an indulgent smile. "I sincerely hope it is. This is a new venture for me and I am expecting my building to be much used to promote it."

"Do you think it has a social impact? By drawing people together?"

"Probably." Tansy watched him smile and thought that he must be satisfied at the turnout for his new venture.

"Why did you buy the building?"

"I've never examined why. A mixture of a good business opportunity in the right place, and some sentiment."

"What about the exhibition itself?"

"I am delighted with it, but have you noticed how, so often on these occasions, everyone talks and they do not allow themselves time to look seriously at the paintings? I don't know how you can change this."

"You could wave a baton, like a conductor, and say 'now we will have fifteen minutes silence for everyone to contemplate Jacob's art'," Tansy laughed.

"Not such a silly idea," Taylor said catching her mood. "Next time I will hire a quartet and announce a time for contemplative viewing."

"That would be novel!" Tansy felt she was monopolising Taylor. "Can I write then? Do you want to see the piece before it is printed? It will only be loosely based on tonight."

"You write whatever you like and I'll look out for your magazine. What was it called again? *Inside and Out*?"

Tansy slipped away and went in search of Reuben. "Who shall I start with?" she asked. Reuben pointed out Kerry, who happened to be standing alone. "She owns the gallery by the town hall."

Tansy explained the outline of her article. Kerry was

enthusiastic. "I think art gives pleasure. My shop would not survive unless people wanted to be surrounded by beautiful things. I'm not sure that I know what good art is but it is irrelevant. Creating is what it is all about, new ideas, seeing things differently. That is what attracts people. What interests me is how a couple, for example, often gravitate towards the same object or picture. Is this because of their shared background, or is it something fundamental, something we don't understand that makes them compatible in the first place. See if you can unravel that in your article."

During her interviews Tansy found that she became the recipient of ideas from people who, she suspected, had never had to verbalise them before. Lauren McGill said she hoped art was a sign that we were civilised, but on reflection she expected that it was the other way around, and that only when we stopped foraging and fighting were we able to use our intellects to create. Tansy feared that Lauren McGill might launch into a quasi-manifesto, but she suddenly gave Tansy a knowing smile and said, "I really think it is important."

Tansy spoke to a teacher who was researching into art therapy in old age, and a mother who was also a social worker who said that she learnt so much from children's artwork that the child could not express otherwise. She was making her way over to a group who, from their ages and by their dress could only be students, to explore their views, when Taylor tapped his glass and called for everyone's attention. No one noticed Craig arrive, nor did they notice that he did not join the crowd who had assembled in the small downstairs room to listen to Taylor's welcome speech and his aspirations for the building. Tansy jotted notes on her pad. When Andrew stepped up to add his thanks for the evening Tansy registered that he was the head of the college and someone she ought to speak to. She was beginning to visualise a theme for her article and she noted some questions to put to him later.

Tansy felt a gentle tug on her elbow. It was Matty.

"Are you bored?" Tansy whispered.

"No. It's strange to see Mum and Dad's paintings all so neatly arranged," she replied, equally quietly.

Tansy bent down slightly so as to be closer to her. "What is it?"

"What are all those red dots?" Matty pointed behind her. "Show me."

Andrew's speech was light-hearted and humorous, absorbing everyone's attention. Tansy and Matty carefully sidled through the press of people to the back of the room.

"There!" Matty stood facing the wall of Jacob's paintings. Every one had a red circular sticker in the bottom right-hand corner.

"A red sticker means that it's been sold," Tansy explained.

"But there are no prices," Matty objected.

They stood together for a few moments staring. Tansy had seen how anxious Matty had been all evening, and surmised that, like Reuben, she worried that her father's paintings might not be appreciated. She knew not to pretend to Matty that this was nothing out of the ordinary. In the case of this evening, it was unexpected and Tansy, too, thought it was curious. "We'll go and ask Reuben."

There was an explosion of clapping as Andrew's speech ended and immediately they were engulfed by people moving away.

"Have you seen the stickers?" Reuben said when they finally located him.

"We came to ask you. Are they for sale?"

"I suppose they could be."

"There are no prices." Tansy said.

"What does it mean?" Matty insisted.

Reuben answered sharply, "How do I know, Matty?"

Tansy gave Matty a sympathetic smile. "We'll find out later."

"I don't understand it. Who's the buyer?" Reuben looked agitated and left them to go and find Taylor. The latter was surrounded by people and he came back to them shaking his head.

"Others are asking the same question but Taylor doesn't have an answer."

Slowly the hall emptied until only Taylor and Jacob's family remained.

It was then that Jacob said, "What about the red dots?" He was clearly amused. "I like your little joke." Without waiting for a reply he placed one hand on Matty's shoulder and his other arm around Deborah and shepherded his family out of the building.

"Excellent show!"

Taylor turned to see Craig saunter over from the rear of the room.

"So you are here! When did you arrive? I never saw you." He hurried across to shake his friend's hand. "And why the little red dots?"

"Looking to the future," Craig told him. "I want first refusal if everything gets turned on its head." Craig waited for Taylor to react.

"Surely you don't think anything will come of it?"

"I don't know, but in my line of work you have to be ahead of the game. If Jacob is prepared to sell, I am prepared to buy, whatever the price."

"You know that girl is going to write about the show. People will speculate," Taylor warned.

Craig laughed. "What is she going to write? The mystery of the little red dots?"

TWELVE

As arranged during the evening of the exhibition, Tansy was to interview Andrew at the college and Kerry at her shop the next morning.

"Can I give you a lift into town, Abi," Tansy asked. Although it was the Easter holidays, Abigail persisted with her regime of leaving early each day and returning home on the last bus.

"I'm all right, thanks."

Tansy was disappointed.

"I have a lunch break at one thirty. You could come to the café." Abigail picked up her bag and headed out of the door.

"I'll make a point of it. Thanks."

Tansy was alone with Deborah. She felt that she should explain herself.

"I've set up some interviews."

"That's nice, dear." Deborah sat down heavily in the nearest chair. "Perhaps you know what is going on?" She looked hopefully at Tansy. "Have you seen the colour of Abi's skin and her dark gaunt eyes? She's not as moody as she used to be, which is a relief I suppose, but I am no closer to finding out why she is like she is. She didn't even come to the exhibition last night."

Tansy felt helpless. "I know."

"Perhaps she'll tell you."

"Perhaps she will."

"I was surprised when she said she would meet you."

"I was surprised too." Tansy wanted to comfort Deborah but without betraying Abigail's trust. "We can only hope."

"Hope?" Deborah looked confused.

"Hope that she will tell someone," Tansy said lamely.

***

At the college Tansy was met by Callum. "Andrew has a golf tournament," he explained.

"It was good of you to meet me when you're on holiday."

"It's a pleasure, and I was free."

As Callum and Tansy walked through the college their footsteps echoed down the corridor. Once they reached the staff room the sounds were muted by the carpeted floor, by the walls which were hung with boards and by the thick blinds which covered the windows. Callum drew up the blinds. The noticeboards were covered in timetables and stickers, and piles of books and papers were stacked up on the desks beside the computers.

"What did you think of the exhibition?" Callum asked as he ushered her to a chair at his desk. Tansy took her time. She had not met Callum during the previous evening and had no indication whether he resented Jacob as an outsider from the college securing the first exhibition. Nor did she yet know her own tastes or trust her own views.

Callum saw her dilemma. "It's not fair to put you on the spot. I'll tell you what I think. Jacob's work is in a league to which we would all aspire. If we could produce work of that calibre I believe none of us would be teaching, even if it did mean scraping a living."

Tansy relaxed. "I'm quite new to this, but I felt excited when I was looking at his paintings."

"That's good enough! But why, if you don't know much

about art, are you employed to write articles on the subject?" Callum's gentle taunt removed any trepidation that Tansy might have felt about answering.

"I am writing on behalf of non-artists," she explained, "I am interested in ideas that colleges are developing. Yours is relatively new isn't it? Was it two years ago?"

"Three," Callum said. "To give you an idea of our projects it's best that I show you around. We'll start with the studios."

One arm of the building that stretched along the estuary led directly from the staff room. In this extension the studios were ranged on either side of a corridor which ended in a large picture window.

"The lighting is better in the studios which face north, but with skylights those on the south side are almost as good, and they benefit in the winter by catching the afternoon sun. We have no problems in the summer. Here on the doors you can see the names of the sponsors."

"Sponsors?"

"When the college was built this extension was not covered by the initial budget so Andrew had the idea of offering studio space. Degree students share their studios with emerging artists or visiting artists who rent them. They are bought or contributed towards, by established artists, local businesses or benefactors. The idea caught on and now we have a studio for each of the final-year students, some of whom share with an artist from outside."

"So when the students leave they can rent a studio if they want to?"

"Certainly. We already have one or two ex-students. Unfortunately most have to move away for work. There's not a lot to offer young people here."

They walked to the end of the corridor and looked out

on the estuary and the hills beyond. "You could just sit here and draw," Tansy commented.

"I have." Callum laughed in self-denigration.

"Is that the sort of painting you do?" Tansy asked. "Landscapes?"

"Not very ambitious, I'm afraid," Callum admitted.

It seemed that Callum was embarrassed and Tansy deflected the conversation. "I wouldn't know. It all seems difficult to me. Can I see the rest of the department?"

It was smaller than Tansy had expected, but Callum explained that other departments such as animation and ceramics were also within the college. "Our department has seventy students all told, even after some have dropped out."

Neither of them mentioned Abigail.

"We have introduced annual shows for each year. Taylor's exhibition hall will give us the space for that. It gives the students more of a focus and the talented ones will find buyers interested in their work."

Tansy wandered from one easel to another and studied the paintings and drawings displayed on the walls. "Their work is very varied. Can you teach all this?"

"I can now. I've been teaching for a while. One idea that Andrew has introduced is an extra diploma so that students can set up classes after school or in the evenings as soon as they graduate."

Tansy took out her pad and starting writing. "I've not heard of that. Jacob will be pleased. Children need to start drawing seriously when they are young, don't they?"

"That's the aim," Callum agreed.

"How do artists make a living?" Tansy looked Callum squarely in the face as she echoed Reuben's challenge.

"To be honest, few do! Mostly we teach. Some manage to paint as well." Callum smiled ruefully and he led her back to the entrance hall. Tansy shook his hand as they parted.

"I've enjoyed it," she told him, pleased with the material she had gathered.

It was only a short walk from the college to the centre of the town and Kerry's shop. It was strange, for someone used to the busy streets in Glasgow, to pass so few people. Tansy presumed that, because the tourist season had not yet started, it gave the impression of being sleepy and old-fashioned. In a few weeks every shop would be busy, every seat in every café would be taken, cars would be circling in search of parking spots, and coaches would be disgorging their passengers.

Tansy was glad to see the town stripped of its glamour, and thought she could feel its essence more vividly. It helped her to understand why Andrew and Callum, and now Taylor, had been drawn to settle here.

Kerry's gallery stood out from among the row of shops that faced the church. Its plain unadorned frontage and large tasteful display windows were stylish and could hold their own in a street of fashionable boutiques. This was praise indeed, as Tansy's assumption that cities held the edge over towns was an unquestioned premise.

"You don't mind if we chat here? I'm on my own today. Have a look around. I'll make some coffee."

That Kerry did not pander to the souvenir-hunting tourist was soon apparent, not only the prices but also the quality of the objects and the care with which they were displayed testified that she aimed at the more affluent customer. She returned carrying two mugs. "I have just realised something. Well, it came to me last night after the exhibition." Kerry looked over her mug and studied Tansy for a few moments. "You're Tansy Witt."

Tansy waited, intrigued.

"You write for *Inside and Out*."

Tansy smiled. "I've been with them for a while."

"You gave me the idea to look out for work by young painters."

"I did?" Tansy found it extraordinary that one of her articles had struck a chord with someone. Was this the power of the written word?

Kerry added excitedly, "And it prompted Gerald to make changes at the college. He's introduced annual shows for all the students. The first-years' show was just before the holidays. I was invited along. Gerald thought that perhaps I might take a gamble and make a purchase."

"Was it worth your while to go and view their work?"

"You can spot talent very early on. Even if I don't offer to buy their work at this stage, I will keep an eye out next year and the year after. Are other colleges doing this?"

"I don't know," said Tansy. "I have yet to visit any. You'll be able to find out in one of my next articles!"

Tansy had time on her hands before meeting Abigail at her café and, returning to the harbour where she had parked her car, changed her shoes for boots, took out a warm jacket and woolly hat and followed the signs to the coastal walk that led along the estuary. She marvelled at her transformation. One year ago, on her first visit, wellington boots were what farmers wore, and going for a country walk was what retired people did, and as for woolly hats, she had only ever seen fashionable beanies.

She came to the end of the gravelled path and ahead was woodland. At this time of the year there was little under-growth and Tansy decided to strike up through the trees. From there she could either go on up the hillside or turn back along the way she had come. Decision making, ever present in the city where even choosing a coffee required looking at five or six options, was reduced here to two.

It was this simplicity that, she suspected, enabled her to return to work refreshed after each visit to Reuben's home. Was it the reverse that prevented Abigail and other young people from leaving their homes, she wondered. Was it the daunting number of decisions and choices?

Later, with all her walking gear removed, Tansy made her way to the fish and chip shop. As soon as she saw her, Abigail closed the till, said a few words to the girl operating the fryer, and disappeared through a door at the back. She emerged wearing a coat to cover her work clothes, and led Tansy to the street. "There's a place I like round the corner," she said, barely meeting Tansy's eyes.

There were only three or four people seated scattered around the café and this gave them some privacy, as did the nebulous background music and the occasional roar of the coffee machine.

Abigail pushed back her hood and Tansy gave her a warm smile. From the wistful look on Abi's face it was clear that she needed a friend, and Tansy risked beginning with a reference to her aborted course. "Is it because you haven't been to classes that you weren't at the exhibition? We missed you."

Abigail did not look upset by her observation and Tansy continued. "No one asked where you were, not even when I met up with Callum this morning. Will you tell them one day?"

"Tell them? That I can't go back? I can't tell anyone until I know what to do next and I don't know what to do, except work. I've let the college down, and I made such an issue of it all with my parents and it has cost them so much and now I have let them down too."

Abigail had raised her voice and heads turned in their direction. Tansy was aware of the attention that they had drawn to themselves and almost without thinking she lowered her voice.

"That is your view," she said steadily and saw a glimmer of a connection in Abigail's eyes. "When you are in the centre of a problem it's difficult to see what others, looking in, are seeing." Abigail did not interrupt. "I see you as someone who can't get out of your predicament on your own."

Abigail sighed. "Every way seems a dead end. Whether I tell my parents, or you, or Reuben, or my tutor, no one can give me an answer as to what I should do. They'll probably tell me to move to another college, but what if it happens again?" She grasped her two hands together fiercely. "And anyway we can't afford it."

Tansy's instinct was to find a way around every problem, even finance, but she held back. "What does David say?"

Abigail's eyes welled with tears. "I've upset his plans too. And his father's. He should be on the boats. To be honest I don't know what I'd do if he did go back, now, I mean."

"Has it ever occurred to you that this might be an unexpectedly good opportunity for David?"

"What do you mean?" Abigail was suddenly disgruntled.

"He'll spend his whole life on the boats. This gives him the chance, just for a short while, to see life on shore. You never know, he might decide that the sea is not for him. Either way you are giving him a choice he would not have had, and one I am certain that his father did not have. We have choices. We are lucky."

"I don't know what my options are," Abigail said flatly, unappeased.

"This is how I see it. You are working. You have David. Are you drawing?"

"When I can on my half-days."

"You can draw."

This seemed so self-evident that Abigail was caught off balance. "I can draw?" she repeated, not understanding.

"You can only not draw at college. So you left, or rather you stopped going." Tansy tried to make it sound logical. "What is more, you have years ahead of you. You don't have to make a decision about your whole life, you have no idea what is around the corner, just be ready for any opportunity."

"Is that what you did?"

"A year ago I wrote one article a month. Now I have enough writing contracts that I only have to work for two days a week at the shop." Tansy thought it might be the right moment to mention the greatest hurdle. "Abi, you need to tell the college."

"I know. There's nothing they can do, but I have a feeling that they were pleased that I chose them and that makes it awkward."

"Because of your connection with Jacob?" Tansy suggested. Abigail nodded.

"But you will tell them?"

"Yes."

A picture of Deborah sitting dejectedly at the kitchen table came to her. "What about your parents? Can you tell them?"

Abigail gave a wan smile. "I don't know if they'd be happy or annoyed. Mum might say I told you so."

Tansy thought it unlikely but felt it was better left unsaid. "Why not tell them but continue working for the moment? It will mean you can spend more time at home."

"I know. I must look as if I'm scuttling away like a startled rabbit." Abigail gave a weak laugh. "I was so scared of anyone knowing what a failure I am." The colour had returned to her face and she looked more animated. "I'm due back at work in five minutes."

"And I have to drive back home. Next time can I see your drawings?"

"If you like."

That evening Tansy recounted her conversation to Reuben.

"I am glad that she has finally come to her senses," he commented. Tansy waited, hoping that he might acknowledge her effort on behalf of the family, but Reuben seemed preoccupied.

"Did you find out anything?" he asked.

"I don't know what you mean."

"About the little red dots?" he said, rather impatiently.

"No."

THIRTEEN

"Hello, Mum. Any lunch going?" Abigail smiled shyly as she entered the kitchen where Deborah was kneading pastry. She had chosen to see her parents during the day because, with Florrie and Matty at school, she would find them alone. Deborah felt relief flooding through her body, looked at her floured hands and then, beaming with happiness, shook them in mock irritation. "I can't even hug you! Give me a moment."

While Deborah was in the scullery rinsing her hands and removing her apron, Abigail took off her jacket and placed it and her shoulder bag on the nearest chair. She waited awkwardly. She was thin but not scrawny, neatly dressed with her hair gleaming. Deborah stood and for a moment surveyed her daughter.

"Come here!" she said, stretching out her arms. Abigail walked towards her as if she had no control. "Tell us what has been going on."

"I'm not going to cry," Abigail said, as tears rolled down her face.

"Shall I call your father?" Deborah asked, giving her an extra hug before releasing her. "Is it very bad?"

"Oh Mum! I'm not pregnant, or on drugs, or broken up with David."

"Or robbed a bank?" Deborah risked lightening the mood.

"I've ruined everything," Abigail announced with a sigh

of despair and gave her mother a wan smile as she ran her hands over her cheeks to clear the rivulets of tears.

"I'll fetch your father. Or do you want to?"

"I'll go." She kissed her mother before leaving through the scullery. She ran down the gravelled path and hurried to the mill. The door stood open and she quickly climbed the stairs.

"That sounds like Abi," Jacob called.

"It's me." She stopped at the top of the stairs. At that moment she realised how much she must have upset her parents by her behaviour. How hurt they must feel that she had not trusted them. "I've come to say sorry."

Jacob wiped his brush automatically on a rag and put it on his palette. He walked slowly across to his daughter. Abigail hung her head. "I'm sorry. I'm so sorry."

"What have you done?" Jacob asked slowly as she buried her head against his chest.

"Let you down," she sobbed.

He stroked her hair and gave her a few minutes. "Let's go and join your mother." He placed a hand on her shoulder and gently steered her towards the steps.

Deborah was grating cheese on to a quiche but stopped as soon as they entered the kitchen. Jacob sat in his armchair while Deborah leant against the range. Abigail perched on the edge of the table facing them. The words tumbled from her as she released all that she had stifled during the past weeks.

At the beginning, she explained, being a student was liberating. There was a dialogue between her and the tutors, instead of the grind to learn facts and the pressure of completing a syllabus. She quickly made friends because she was one of the few who lived locally and she could help them. Slowly it changed. She didn't go to parties or pubs and there weren't many other students like her who weren't interested. She took the course seriously and this seemed to irritate one or two and soon after that the snide comments began. She tried to ignore them and concentrate on her work but she was more and more in the minority. "Until I thought that I might as well be working at home. Even the tutors seemed to sense that if they made any comment on my work it would be interpreted as favouritism." She could not bring herself to blame the preparations for her father's exhibition for its part in exacerbating her predicament.

When she had finally exhausted her litany of miseries, she looked from one parent to the other awaiting their verdict.

"Abi, none of this matters except for the misery you've put yourself through," Deborah was the first to speak and then she directed her gaze towards Jacob.

Slowly he added, "I suppose you want to know what to do next?"

"You don't mind? That I dropped out?" Abigail studied her parents' faces in disbelief.

"The prerogative of youth, Abi," Jacob pronounced, and Abigail waited for Deborah to state her opinion.

"You know my views on colleges. I can see how you felt, having insisted on going it was bound to be awkward to tell us that you had dropped out."

"So it's all right?"

Neither parent answered but Abigail did not need to be told. The tears fell gently onto her lap and she did not attempt to brush them away.

Deborah gave her time and then said, "Come here!" Abigail went across and felt her mother's arm around her shoulders.

"And what to do now?" Jacob asked but did not wait for her to reply and proceeded to supply the answer.

"Nothing!"

"Nothing?" Abigail sniffed and wiped her eyes with the palms of her hands.

"Just keep doing what you are doing until the right moment or opportunity presents itself. Tell me, where is David working? You say he left the boats."

"With Lauren. Lauren McGill." Jacob and Deborah showed no signs of recognising the name. "She's our MSP, you know!" Abigail smiled, at last, at the isolated cocoon in which her parents lived.

***

At the office of Lauren McGill, David was sifting through the in-tray on his desk looking for any correspondence that needed an urgent response. Lauren insisted that every communication was acknowledged within a week and David wanted some instructions while she was available.

"Have you got your diary up to date? I could answer this for you," David offered. "It's the degree show at McFarlane's."

"Could you refuse any requests for the last week of June? That week is manic in Edinburgh. Also, I can't do the fourth and fifth of July because of Tynwald, and the sixth, too, as I will be travelling back." David began to divide the pile into two and Lauren moved towards her own office. "You know Tynwald?" she called over her shoulder.

"The Isle of Man! My Dad goes there every year. They have the longest-running parliament. It's been going for a thousand years," David said smugly and Lauren turned to show that she was impressed.

"Now find out what those three legs circling in the air symbolise. It's on all their letterheads." She closed her door and left David alone.

Lauren had a matronly figure, was always smartly dressed in a jacket and skirt, rarely trousers, and commanded respect because she worked hard. Her commitment to local people was as visible now as it had been during her years on the school council and then as a councillor. She was a rewarding person to have as an employer. David suspected that she would not suffer fools and he had discovered that it was best to admit his ignorance if he was not certain of a procedure. He enjoyed his work and although it had not proved to be what he expected, he was not sure, now, what he did expect.

When David told his father about his job, John had one proviso. "Lauren's a good sort, nearly a local, she came from Kirklington, and even when she worked at McGill's butchers with her husband she did a decent job. Probably, like most of us, she decided it was best for them not to live and work together. Maybe she outgrew it and needed a greater challenge. But no politics in the house, David, keep it in the office!"

"It doesn't feel political, Dad. We just help people. Anybody. Lauren's more like a social worker. This person needs the council to put in a ramp, another needs help with the rules for a bed and breakfast and another wants their single-track road tarmacked. I expect it's different in the parliament."

"Watch out!" John laughed, "or you'll be going into politics!"

"Don't worry, I'll be back on the boats by the end of the year."

"You will?"

David was grateful that his father had until now hidden his anxiety, but he was in no hurry to return to the sea. This interlude was all the better for being finite, and he liked having his own desk, making phone calls on people's behalf, and discovering life beyond his narrow environs. He also appreciated his free time, more than he ever did in his school-days, and his moments with Abigail. She really was less tearful and becoming fun to be with again.

"David, can you type out these letters for me?" Lauren came through from her office still reading the top copy. She handed them to David who put them on a pile and then she said, "Any luck with our three-legged man?"

"The Treskelion? No one knows the origin. Probably a pagan symbol. The legs are golden and spurred. It seems to symbolise that whatever you do to them, they will land on their feet."

"That's not a bad motto," Lauren decided. "Never let them get you down. Remember that when things get tough. You could say that's been my motto but I didn't know it."

When David finished his work he placed everything on his desk ready for the next week. He had developed a routine: switch off the computer, file any loose papers, replace pens, pencils and markers, push his chair under his desk and pick up his jacket from the back of the chair. Today it was also his job to close the office, which he did conscientiously, switching off the lights and shutting the door to Lauren's office. David was turning the key in the lock when he was aware of someone standing on the corner close to the building.

"Abi?" David experienced a mix of emotions, from fear that a new crisis had arisen for him to cope with, to hope that this unexpected appearance presaged a return to a normal relationship.

Abigail responded with one of her once familiar grins. David waited for her as he put the key carefully into his jacket pocket. She ran, her hair flying behind her, free from the austere ponytail that she had recently adopted, and almost unbalanced David with the force of her embrace.

David held her, not for weeks had he felt able to show such feelings. Abigail's had been locked up and there had been no opening for David to initiate any contact.

Clutching his hand fiercely she dragged him away from the office. "Let's go somewhere and talk!" she said happily. David was light-headed from the unexpected turn of events, and was prepared to follow wherever she suggested. "Or just go for a walk. I can't tell you what I feel like now I've told Dad and Mum, David." She turned towards him with a look of incredulity, and walked backwards for a few steps. "Neither of them were annoyed with me." Then she was suddenly contrite and took his hand again, walking in step. "I know you told me this. I should have believed you, but I had to do it on my own."

David kissed her playfully. "There was no reason for you to believe me. I just hoped. That's all."

"Well at least you trusted them, which is more than I did."

They walked in no particular direction until they found themselves by the harbour. The tide was rising and there was activity on several of the boats as they prepared for a night of fishing. David knew the men and wondered if they thought he lacked the courage to go out with his father. Unconsciously he tightened his grip on Abigail's hand.

"You can go back to the boats now," Abigail said.

"No. Not yet," he answered.

Angrily Abigail broke away from him and began to walk ahead. "I'm all right now. I can manage. I don't need you here all the time."

David fell silent, trying to process the import of her

remark. "I'm not going back to the boats, not yet," he said grimly, and then to shake her he added, "and it's not because of you."

"Then why?" Abigail stopped and turned towards him. "What possible reason could you have?"

"Because, Abi, I like the job." He hoped she would understand. "And I like being with you."

"And I like being with you," Abigail repeated, softening quickly in response to this unexpected declaration.

They continued along the harbour towards the coastal path without speaking.

"Shall we climb through the woods to the top of the hill?" David asked.

"I love that walk."

FOURTEEN

Although The Artist's Town had an air of prosperity, with shops flaunting modern frontages, cafés furnished with shiny chrome tables and counters, streets with hanging baskets on every telegraph pole and fresh paint on their traditionally built houses, the same could not be said of their hostelries. The hotels in the town suffered from years of neglect and lack of investment. The change in drinking laws and the availability of alcohol in supermarkets at every hour except before twelve on a Sunday had reduced the numbers who drank in pubs and hotels. In many instances the quality of the food was poor because of the competition for good chefs by the more progressive hotels in the district.

Fortunately the old timers, those who had lived in the town for most of their lives, failed to notice the shortcomings in décor and service, and for them the camaraderie and the atmosphere were unchanged. This had the advantage of reserving these otherwise redundant hotels for the local people. There was always someone perched on a bar stool, or sitting at a table nursing a drink with whom they would have at least a nodding acquaintance. Time was not at a premium and one pint could last an evening. Alternatively, a night might develop into a party, or even a fight, given certain individuals.

It was to one such pub that Craig had invited John, Callum and Taylor. They arrived within a few minutes of each other to find Craig already ensconced with his drink at a table with vacant chairs. The four men had, the week before, returned from their annual trip to the Isle of Man. Each of them was aware that the news that had been presented in embryo the year before was in some form to become concrete and incorporated into Tynwald law in a few weeks' time. Craig was anxious for them to meet to discuss the implications for each of them. He had excluded Andrew, not because he had any unkind or underhand motive but because he did not want to compromise his position.

"Good to see you again. Here's to John for a great weekend!" They raised their glasses and John raised his in return.

"Couldn't do it without you!" he grinned.

Craig opened with the question that all of them had been turning over in their minds for most of that week. "What do we do now?"

Taylor was the first to respond. "I've been trying to imagine what the islanders who are in the know will be doing before July fifth."

"July fifth?" John asked.

"Tynwald. When the proposal to limit ownership of works of art to one hundred years becomes law," Taylor explained. "What will we all do? What would I do? I would start renegotiating contracts, but I would need to do it without raising suspicion or scaring people to move to other brokers."

"So what have you done, or plan to do?" John pressed him.

"Those on the Isle who own valuable paintings of over one hundred years old will have to decide whether to keep them or give them to their national gallery. However, the astute will be selling them, anywhere they can, fast, knowing that they only have a month. They are the ones who will be coming to me to renegotiate their insurance policies."

"Won't you lose a whole lot of money?" Callum asked.

"Probably not in the long run. Very soon, although the premiums on the older pictures will be reduced, as the market reacts to the new situation the premiums on recent purchases will increase. As I see it, this has opportunities for all of us."

John waded in with another question. "Who determines the hundred years?"

"It seems that the moment a new painting goes on the market it will be chipped. The grey area is around those paintings in circulation which have been sold within the last hundred years. Verification will then be by a bill of sale from records kept in auction houses, and if there is no record, then they will be chipped on the day that they are put up for sale."

"So even if a painting was done fifty years ago but has never been put up for sale, it will be considered new?"

"There's no other way. Lucky for the ones who have been harbouring paintings," Craig observed.

"What I don't understand," Callum said, "is who is going to buy these new paintings?" Craig had been waiting for this question because it directly affected him, and he and Eoin had speculated about it long and hard the previous week. "We see it like this. There is a lot of money invested in art, just as people invest in property or shares. That money will still go into art but the emphasis will shift. It will be far more of a gamble and buyers will have to rely on their intuition. Previously, to invest safely, a buyer would purchase the work of a recognised artist. No matter how bizarre the painting, once it is an accepted phenomenon, once everyone is talking about it, it is a reasonably safe bet that, if bought, the painting will only increase in value. If the older paintings become valueless, the market will have to turn to the contemporary."

John was still puzzled. "Why should anyone pay substantial amounts for a new painting when it will ultimately be valueless?"

Craig answered, "In my opinion people will always want to buy paintings. People want to see, or preferably own, valuable and beautiful things. If I were to buy a stunning new painting now, on the Isle, in due course someone will want to own it and probably be prepared to pay more. It will last their lifetime, and their offspring's lifetime. During that time it will maintain or increase its value. No one worries what will happen in fifty years' time. At present we have this mindset, this idea, that it must increase in value and that is the main criterion for art. If I buy a wonderfully crafted desk or chair, I don't buy it because it might sell for more once I'm dead. I buy it because it's a wonderfully crafted desk or chair. The Isle of Man legislation will change established trading."

"How do you mean?" Callum asked. "How does anything that happens on that tiny island affect anywhere else?"

"Do you think that other countries are going to pass up the chance to accrue a regular income from a commodity where until now money changes hands, often in offshore investment accounts, with little going to the Treasury? They will soon copy this law. You'll see," Craig answered.

"Also," added Taylor, "there's the political angle. In this way Tynwald is showing that they can divert money into the pockets of living artists, while coincidentally, and this is their ultimate aim, tax that money. It's a win-win situation."

"Except for those who have squirrelled away their money

into Old Masters and saleable artists as a way of saving or investing," John commented.

"There are always losers. You could own a house worth two million and a motorway could be constructed past your front door. The ivory you own is now worthless because sales are illegal, the masterpiece you own could be a fake, your land could be compulsorily purchased. It's an uncertain world, and art investment is a gamble. It's just that this time they are unlikely to see the crash coming."

"But only on the island," Callum insisted.

"I think not," Craig repeated. "It's my guess that we will see it adopted by our parliament before the year is out."

No one said anything while each contemplated how their career would be affected. Only John was free from any involvement. Callum, Taylor and Craig each realised that the results of a change of emphasis in the market would do none of them any harm, and might possibly be to their advantage. With the money accrued from selling his present stock of traditional paintings with which he would then buy modern paintings from unsuspecting sellers ahead of the legislation, Craig predicted that he would certainly break even and possibly make a profit. Callum could see advantages for his students, and Taylor was confident that after an initial dip, his trade would rally.

"I've just remembered," John broke the silence. "David said that his boss, Lauren, is going to Tynwald. She'll be there when they announce the new law."

"So she could be the person who would introduce the idea to parliament. The success of our plans is based on the assumption that other countries follow the precedent set by Tynwald. I wonder if she will see the significance," Craig said sceptically.

"If she doesn't, David will soon put her wise to it, I'll

make certain of that!" John assured them.

Their conversation had given each of them food for thought and while Craig walked back with John, he voiced his misgivings.

"It's all very well saying what I would do in the event that these changes materialise, but it's quite different facing up to reality. What if no other parliament follows the course set by Tynwald?"

John was surprised to hear Craig disclose that he was not as optimistic as they had been led to believe by his bullish assessment of the situation. Craig was at the mercy of a market over which he had no control, much as John was at the mercy of the sea, but, in his opinion, he, Craig and Taylor showed a similar personality trait. Each tended to react to a challenge positively and none were frightened into inaction by the unexpected. John's work threw up the unexpected on every trip, and it was not only the sea that caused problems; his crew could be even more demanding, but he trusted that he could surmount any maritime difficulty. He did, however, appreciate the enormity of the new scenario that was facing Craig in his line of work.

"I would not like to be in your shoes," John commented. "The sea may be unpredictable but at least its unpredictability is confined to the weather. I'm unlikely to have to face something that no one has faced before, unlike you," he joked.

"Fortunately I am not so old that I can't adapt, nor am I in the early stages of a business where a fickle market could be ruinous," Craig philosophised.

John admired his attitude but expressed his own doubts, "You wouldn't want to quit and try something else?"

"I'm hooked I'm afraid," Craig admitted. Then he shrugged and a mischievous look crossed his face. "I'm intrigued, to be honest."

John had confidence in Craig's ability to ride an upheaval and wanted to hear his strategy. "What do you plan to do?"

"I need to do an about-turn on how I buy. I have a month's advance on the rest of the field and I need to use it. You don't fancy risking a few quid and buying an undiscovered masterpiece or two, or even a whole artist's collection?"

John wondered if he had someone in mind and looked studiedly at Craig, trying to ascertain if he was serious. "Perhaps," he answered cautiously. "I'll let you know."

***

Taylor mulled over the information that he had gleaned from their conversation. The visit to the Isle of Man and his subsequent conversations with Craig and Callum had re-energised Taylor, who had felt poorly motivated since his wife had died. He had searched for a way of eradicating the memories of their time together, which when they resurged were so destructive. He disliked the self-pity that they awoke in him and he endeavoured to suffocate them with action. Every morning was an effort, every evening he approached with dread, and the nights were wakeful, but now that he had a project, these gloomy moments were taking second place. These events had connected him with people again. The awkwardness of carrying his past into all encounters could now be banished since they had a common topic and a common challenge and for the first time since he had been on his own, Taylor experienced a sense of purpose.

Jacob's exhibition had prompted Taylor to re-evaluate his gallery and as a result he had nurtured the idea of altering the way people look at paintings. Art exhibitions required physical stamina. It was possible to enjoy concerts, plays, dance and opera while sedentary; only in galleries were viewers asked to stand, and jostle for a viewing position, and walk for an hour or more. Taylor was in the process of redesigning a part of his gallery so that his visitors could enjoy his exhibits without being obliged to stand, and had already contacted his architect with a rough sketch. He envisaged a staircase leading down from the upper floor to a theatre below. This theatre would be circular in shape and would encompass half of the ground floor and house around thirty seats. There would be an outer and an inner wall with a window cut into the inner of the walls. Between the two walls would be a track along which a screen, with paintings attached, would travel. One by one the paintings would appear at the open window. The timing and lighting would be controlled either manually, in the manner of an old-fashioned slide show, or pro-grammed to operate automatically. Background music could be added if Taylor considered that silence made the experience uncomfortable. A simple air-conditioning system was the final requirement.

Taylor was excited by his innovative idea, although he was prepared to concede that the idea had originated from a comment by that young journalist. Taylor made a mental note to ask Andrew how he could contact Tansy once his theatre was in action; the girl might like to write about his invention in an article for her magazine.

Callum was energised by the prospect of a surge of interest in contemporary artists. Suddenly the notion of painting, that had been dormant for years, became attractive and compelling and he wondered why he had been so dismissive of his talent and so easily prepared to submit to the generally accepted view that the old and trusted was more desirable than the new and untried. Callum made a pledge to paint regularly and see if he could not, after all, become the artist that he aspired to be and go on improving long after his teaching days were over. He wondered if his modest paintings might attract some speculative buyer and allowed himself to imagine his paintings hanging in an exhibition of his own.

***

The next week in the staff room, Callum looked at the list that Andrew had compiled of invitees for the degree show. "I see that you have invited Jacob this year. Do you think he will come?"

"It's a gesture," Andrew replied, "he must know by now that his daughter has dropped out, but I want to keep our links with him."

"Abigail's gone?" Callum exclaimed.

"I thought you must have known," Andrew excused himself. "She came to see me. She was quite distressed."

"I noticed that she didn't exhibit any of her work at the Easter show, but as she's not one of my students I didn't think to ask why."

"Too much pressure, I fear. From us, from expectations from other students, on herself, and then there's her father's reputation."

"I can understand that," Callum said thoughtfully. "Did you see any of her work?"

"Only her folio before she arrived. The one she presented when she applied. Gerald and I were both impressed."

"It's a pity." Callum continued to read the list of invitees.

"If you can think of anyone we could co-opt to our Friends committee to increase our number of patrons, add them too." Andrew was always content to trust Callum with the details. "There seems to be a move afoot to encourage new artists, from what I understand."

"Is there a move?" Callum wondered aloud.

"To do what?"

"To encourage new artists." Callum did not assume that Andrew had yet heard about the Isle of Man statutes.

"I read an article by that Tansy Witt. It made convincing reading, and in our situation, if there is a shift to recognise new artists it'll give our place a boost. However, I can't imagine how it could be achieved."

Callum did not comment for fear that he would reveal what he knew. Instead he said, "She had a good manner, that girl. She seemed genuinely interested in the work of the college. I must look out for the next issue of her magazine, we might have a mention." He then remembered that Andrew had been talking about Abigail. "What is she going to do? Jacob's daughter."

"She was not clear. Nothing for the moment. We'll hear from John in time."

"Have there been many drop-outs from this year?"

"Only one other. The usual. Pregnant. Oh! And there was a boy who barely lasted two weeks. We never did fathom out what happened to him. He was not from around here. In all it wasn't too bad."

But Callum knew that Andrew was disappointed, he disliked losing any student, because it reflected on his decision making and he would particularly regret the loss of a potential star.

"Would you accept her back? If she took a year out, for example?"

"Like a shot," Andrew answered animatedly.

"Perhaps that is all she needs." Callum hoped for Andrew's sake that Abigail would return and was glad to know that Andrew had left the door open for her.

FIFTEEN

"Hello, Lauren. How was the Isle of Man?"

Lauren thought, not for the first time, what a charming and well-mannered lad she had employed. Although David might be as uninterested in her trip as her husband, Bill, at least he did not greet her with, "Was it worth it, then?"

"Not a bit what I expected. We were asked to bring a stone with us." Lauren gauged correctly that this would spark David's curiosity. "I took one that we've had in the house for years, one of the boys brought it home from the beach at Saint Ninian's Cave."

"The ones with a cross on them."

Lauren nodded happily. "The stone was a perfect egg shape. The Manx people have created a millennium garden and the feature with a cairn of stones from all over the world symbolises unity and creates a common link."

"It could do that," David agreed. "So you had a stone in your handbag! I'm surprised it got through security. It's nice to think that one of our stones is in a prominent place on the Isle of Man."

"Until it gets buried," Lauren laughed.

How could Lauren explain the contrasting impressions of the past forty-eight hours between her pressurised modern life and the ancient ceremony that she had just witnessed. At the airport Lauren had been processed in dumb acceptance as usual and found her seat on the plane as she had on many previous occasions. However, the aeroplane had not been ten minutes in the air before she felt the thrill of an entirely new experience, one she likened to that of an astronaut viewing the Earth from space. Below her was a landscape that she had not previously seen from the air, yet was so familiar and had such significance that she became mesmerised by the view from her window. Lauren watched with increasing excitement as her country, her towns, and her villages passed beneath the wings with the sunlight highlighting the river courses, and the clouds forming patterns on the hills. The sensation was physical, as if she could reach out to touch the land and follow the brain-like contours of the coastline with a fingertip.

From the air the strategic position of the Isle of Man was evident. It was located, fitting like the key piece in a jigsaw, equidistant from all of the component parts of the British mainland and Ireland. Lauren made no apology to her absent audience for classing Ireland as one country as she sensed the ancient geography beyond the present and its politics.

As the plane touched down, Lauren stepped back in time but could not place the era. Within minutes she was greeted by a member of the House of Keys, presented with a posy and ushered into a waiting car. She was used to facing situations alone. After a half-hearted attempt to entice Bill to join her, she accepted defeat and had to admit that by being on her own she was able to immerse herself in the old world offered to her, without reference to family or her workday environment.

Lauren had a surprisingly large suitcase for her short sojourn, but the invitation included several official functions, each advising a different dress code. Her host indicated that she had a short time to change before the evening cocktail party.

The hotel room was not modernised, with the exception, which did nothing to enhance its overall aspect, of the insertion of an en-suite shower in one corner. Her room was reminiscent of some that she and Bill had stayed in during the early years of their marriage. Net and brocade curtains hung in the windows under heavy pelmets, and the carpet, bedspread and cushions all shrieked modernity consistent with the fashion of twenty years ago. Lauren had time to hang up her clothes, wash and make up her face, and put on her useful little blue dress. She chose blue rather than ubiquitous black because black was so dreary even if it did flatter the figure, and the 'little' was wishful thinking. Happy with her attire she descended the stairs.

Many of the guests were already assembled and waiting in the hallway. Lauren found a space and stood alone without any awkwardness, certain that no one else would be familiar with proceedings and assuming that they would be instructed where to go and when. In this she was correct. A coach drove them the short distance to the Lord Lieutenant's house where Guides and Scouts and other uniformed personnel offered drinks and canapés. Small talk was unforced since they all had a common topic in Tynwald, besides which entertainment was provided in the form of a classical quintet, a brass band, and the obligatory speeches. The hour passed quickly and Lauren could remember, when on the coach heading back to the hotel, only a conversation with an air cadet who offered to refill her glass. This young girl said that she and the other cadets would be lining the route for the procession to the hill on the following day, and Lauren promised to look out for her.

Dinner was spent in the company of a member from the Iceland Parliament, who she was pleased to note was also on his own, a member from the House of Keys and his wife, and another woman representing a group of islands that she did not know existed, somewhere in the vicinity of Denmark. Conversation was somewhat desultory, whether due to the soporific effect of the champagne, or the hindrance of language, or merely the weariness of a collection of overworked parliamentarians, Lauren could not decide. In her case it was a combination of all those factors.

Breakfast was a solitary affair, no one seeming to seek out others to share their table. Lauren then joined the other guests who were exhorted to be ready in the hall by half past nine. Hats were obligatory for the ladies and suits or tailcoats for the men. Today was the most important in the Manx calendar for the islanders. The TT races, although more famous, were predominantly an attraction for outsiders.

The coach took the guests to the millennium garden, where they admired the flowers and the arboretum around its periphery, and where they had the opportunity to add their stones to the rapidly growing pile. To fortify them for the extended ceremony ahead, the guests were offered coffee and tea under a marquee on the edge of Tynwald field, before being invited by their hosts to follow them to the chapel.

All the guests had to be in their seats in St John's Chapel a full half an hour before the service began. Every seat was punctiliously allocated and Lauren was delighted to find that her pew was near the front of the balcony, almost in the centre, and as the balcony was directly above the west door of the chapel, she had an uninterrupted view of the aisle leading to the chancel along which all the dignitaries processed. She could check their identities in the order of service, a comprehensive booklet which was slipped into the back flap of their official brochure.

While the organist played a medley of uplifting pieces, many familiar to Lauren in whose early life regular church-going had been a fixture, conversation was hushed and Lauren was able to absorb the atmosphere of the occasion. Led by a woman carrying a sword, the procession consisted of men in wigs and gold-trimmed robes, men and women in bright scarlet uniforms, men in top hats, men and the occasional woman representing the judiciary, the clergy, and the all-important legislature and House of Keys. The Lieutenant Governor, who was the figurehead for the ceremony, was the last to arrive, resplendent in full military uniform.

All this pageantry was played out against a backdrop of turquoise-blue paintwork, dark wood pews, white rafters and arched beams. The architecture was designed to focus sunlight on to the semi-circular domed recess which formed the alcove for the altar. The stage was set for the solemn Anglican service.

Lauren wondered how much of the experience she would be able to convey when she was back in the office, but she was pleased that David appeared genuinely intrigued.

"What about Tynwald? What is so different?"

"The path from the chapel to the hill where Tynwald is held was strewn with layers of dried grass which was lined on both sides by uniformed children and adults. I concentrated on not going over on my ankles in my high-heeled shoes, or losing my hat in the breeze and so I missed the young cadet that I had promised to recognise. The hill is a man-made grassy mound in four tiers with a white circular tent and a flag on the topmost tier. It has a medieval atmosphere. We sat on chairs in a grassed moat surrounding the hill and behind us were seats for the public. There were rituals which appointed people to various positions and then they promulgated, that's the word that they use, the

laws. They are read first in Manx and then in English."
Lauren opened her bag and rummaged around until she
extracted a booklet. "We were given this with a shortened
version of the laws. Towards the end people came forward
to present their petitions. I'd have loved to have seen
those." Lauren handed him the booklet.

David ran his eyes down the list of laws which had been
drawn up during the year and could now be enforced.
"*Stattys ny Moddee.* Dogs Act," David read aloud. There
were a number of laws beginning with the word *Stattys.*
"*Moddee* is dog," he deduced triumphantly.

"Good word!" Lauren agreed. "I'm afraid I wasn't really
concentrating on the laws. I spent my time studying
everyone on the hill and listening to the Manx."

"*Ratchyn Raaidey* is road race," David went on to inform
her.

"Indeed? To be honest it is all a haze, but I would not
have missed it. Afterwards we went back to the chapel."

"More processions?"

"This time to sign the laws. A sort of court."

Lauren disappeared, shutting the door. There would be
plenty of correspondence awaiting her in her office.

David was up to date with his work. He read through the
new Acts only stopping when he saw '*Stattys obbyr Ellyn
keesh*'. The translation told him that the Act made provision for works of art over one hundred years old. David
was amused. It seemed like a mythical country, like Angria
or Rivendell, whose quaint laws were of little relevance to
anyone else.

David's mind moved swiftly ahead to plans that he,
Reuben, Tansy and Abi were making for the upcoming
music festival. They needed a tent but he had been unable
to borrow one since everyone he knew was intending to be
there, and he started to search on the internet.

Lauren, coming back from her office, looked over his shoulder. "You need a tent? We've got one in the attic. Don't hesitate to ask if ever you think I can help." David could not disguise his disbelief. He could not imagine Lauren in jeans and an anorak cooking burnt sausages amongst the midges and the ever-hovering Scottish drizzle.

It seemed that Lauren could read his thoughts – as clearly as if he had spoken. "We used to camp, you know," she said, giving him a conspiratorial wink.

SIXTEEN

Taylor's gallery had been undergoing some interior alterations and in advance of re-opening he decided that he would contact Tansy. She had struck him as a level-headed and efficient young girl and he had watched approvingly the respectful and unobtrusive manner that she employed when she had interviewed people at his party.

Taylor's spirits lifted as Tansy, smiling and eager, shook his hand.

"Can I give you a story? Would you like to write about my plans for this building?" Taylor was touched to see Tansy's face light up. "You might be interested, not least because it was your comments at the exhibition which sparked these ideas."

"What were they? I would be so grateful for a story." Her childish fervour touched Taylor, who feared that she was too vulnerable to be a really ambitious journalist. He wondered how she would respond if she had an adverse reaction to one of her stories. Fortunately she had chosen a section of the media that was relatively uncontroversial.

The theatre, as Taylor was calling his circular viewing room, was midway through its construction but this was sufficient for Tansy to grasp his concept. She took out her notebook and pen and took down details as she listened to Taylor explain the way the viewing wall worked and how he had adapted the original design.

"We realised that if the inner wall was plywood and not brick it would be more versatile, and we could assemble and disassemble it in sections. We could have access to the moving screen, to the track if there were faults, and we could vary the size of the viewing window." Tansy asked about lighting, seating and soundproofing and Taylor drew out a large drawing from under his desk. "This is to scale, and the details are more or less correct."

"Can I have a copy? Could you send me one?"

"Why not? You can use it in your article."

If she connected her flippant remarks at Jacob's exhibition with the auditorium that she now witnessed, she made no comment except to congratulate Taylor on the quality of the workmanship and the speed of construction.

"I can take no credit for that but you could give the local builders a recommendation."

"I'm grateful for your time. People are so generous when I'm the beneficiary."

"I don't see it as an altruistic gesture," Taylor replied, "I am just content to help a young girl who is setting out on her career."

However, Taylor had another agenda. "What do you know about the Art Act?" he asked. Since much of the information that he, Callum and Craig had heard had been hearsay from Eoin he approached the subject cautiously.

"Only that the Tynwald have put one on their statute book," Tansy answered. "David told me about it and said that it might give me a subject for an article."

Taylor nodded. "It might. However, it would be advisable to secure the facts."

"How?" Tansy persisted, mystified.

"From what we understand they are virtually confiscating all paintings over a hundred years old."

She registered the enormity of the impact of such a story

and then she breathed out heavily. "But it's only on the Isle of Man."

Taylor left it at that. It was not up to him to predict the onward effect of the legislation, even if he had already made some provision for the likelihood that it would cross the water. Although he was hesitant about revealing the rumblings that they had uncovered in the art world on the Isle, he was prepared to direct her to Craig. If Craig divulged more of the story, then it would not be on his conscience if Tansy happened to face any repercussions.

"I'll give you the name of a dealer who lives in Edinburgh. He might fill you in on the developments in the Isle of Man."

By mid-morning the next day she was on the bus to Edinburgh.

"There's a café in St Andrew's Square," Craig had instructed her. "It's opposite the entrance to the bus station. I'll meet you there. I'll recognise you. I saw you at Andrew's gallery." Tansy felt herself blush and was glad that they were speaking on the telephone. "You were the only woman wielding a notebook that night!" he added.

In the café, after a few conventional preliminaries, Craig asked her, "What did Taylor tell you about the Art Act?"

Tansy recounted as much as she understood. "Taylor told me that it was on the statute books of the Tynwald, but I can't see how it can be enforced anywhere other than on the island."

"That's the point! The legislation could have far-reaching effects. It could affect us here. If that happened then it is a big story. If you were the first on the scene you might even sell it to a national newspaper. That would launch a new career path for you if you wanted it."

Beside the café an exhibition of eco-friendly technology had been erected and occupied a large area of the square;

every inch of the grass surrounding it was appropriated by office workers escaping into the sun for their lunch hour. It struck Tansy that Scotland's rain did not fall here as often as it did in the West. Although such a short distance from Glasgow, Tansy felt that she had entered a different country. Glasgow's buildings bore down on the streets, which were narrow and more congested, yet there was an overall feeling of purpose. In her imagination the architecture and the people were brushed with shades of grey and both spelt industry. There was a sense of conformity in the way people were striving to earn a living, yet always in the background a cheerful camaraderie. She found in Glasgow a readiness in people to communicate that she found lacking on her few visits to Edinburgh. The inhabitants of Edinburgh were so diluted by the year-round influx of foreigners who flocked to the city that, although the cosmopolitan mix intrigued her, she never experienced the cohesion that drew her to Glasgow.

St George's Square in the centre of Glasgow was dwarfed by comparison to the grand design of the centre of Edinburgh, many of whose streets were laid out in a perfect grid and graced with classical architecture, yet she felt intimidated by its stately majesty.

"Do you like living in Edinburgh?" Tansy asked. Not having followed Tansy's train of thought, Craig was caught off guard.

"I had, until recently, to live here as a matter of necessity. I like it well enough, but when you've been brought up in a rural town there is a sense of loneliness. Edinburgh has its own community, obviously, and becoming part of a place takes time. So, yes, I do like it here, but I would prefer to be back where I started. But you're here to find a story. I'll give you the background to it, how it all began a year ago when Taylor, Callum and I went with John to the TT races, then you'll have to go and speak to Eoin."

***

At Glasgow station Tansy studied the noticeboard which loomed over the large forecourt, informing travellers of departures and arrivals. Around her people walked in every direction while she stood searching, like a lone tree in a storm, for information about her platform. Suddenly, with suitcases trundling behind them, people surged forwards and Tansy registered that Lancaster was one of the destinations. It was the west coast train and from the number of travellers ahead of her, this was a popular route.

Although Tansy had travelled a fair amount, all her journeys had been abroad and her most common method of transport was by air. This trip to England, by train and ferry, was in its way a much greater adventure. There was no one to check that she had arrived, or taken her seat, or caught the ferry. She had to be self-reliant and was truly independent. She had an intoxicating moment when she realised that she could go anywhere at any time and all she had to do was to step on a train.

However, first she had to find her reservation. The seat beside hers was already occupied by a neatly dressed man in his thirties who was peering anxiously at his computer with his phone to his ear. As Tansy sat down her neighbour finished his phone call but did not raise his eyes from his screen and she deduced that she would not be expected to speak to him. Tansy took her book from her bag and surveyed her fellow passengers. As expected there was a mix, including a group of women in undersized pink t-shirts and semi-transparent white trousers, who were creating quite a commotion as they settled into their seats with a bundle of helium balloons and a stack of alcopops. Tansy put her head down and began to read in earnest, hoping that she would reach Lancaster before the group became too boisterous. She had seen enough of hen parties to distrust that they would have consideration for those around them.

After an hour of nondescript terrain, Tansy's attention was caught by some distant hills. Would the famous Lake District be distinctively Cumbrian, she wondered? As passengers changed, so did the accents, and the style of clothes, and the further south she travelled the more aware she became that England was different. There was so much unexpected variety. By the time Tansy changed to the branch line to Heynsham, she vowed that this was to be only the first of many trips south of the border that she intended to make. There must be so much more to explore.

It felt strange to board a ferry holding only a ticket. Wherever she had travelled, Tansy had needed a passport. Here she felt as alien as in any of the countries that she had visited with her parents, and yet all she needed was a paper ticket.

Douglas, when the ferry drew into the harbour, felt almost familiar, after the landscape of northern England and her overnight stay in Lancaster. The rows of solidly built hotels and guest houses which lined the harbour and continued into the town itself were not unlike the Scottish ports. Indeed, geographically, Douglas was not so far away, there was simply no means of crossing by sea, the shortest route, from the southern Scottish coast to the Isle.

Eoin was to meet her from the ferry because there was only a two-hour window before the boat returned to the mainland. He was one of only a few waiting to meet the hoards of passengers who descended from the ferry down the gangplank like sheep being unloaded from a haulage truck. He stood, conspicuous in a tweed three-piece suit and brogues, at some distance from the railings, seeming bemused by the disparate group of people visiting his Isle, and Tansy had no difficulty in identifying him.

"Welcome! Hello!" Eoin took Tansy's hand in both of his and she suspected that if etiquette allowed he would have engulfed her in a bear hug. All Eoin's movements were strong and expansive. "Here we have a jewel of an island," Eoin waved his arm in a sweep to encompass the entire coastline. "If only I could take you around the whole place! Another time! You must be famished. My shop is a few hundred yards from the dock and we can have a bit of lunch on the way." They walked a short distance up the street until Eoin stopped in a doorway.

"We'll find a table in here."

It was obvious that Eoin was a regular. Immediately a young lad stood beside their table with his pad in hand. "The usual?" he asked Eoin.

Eoin's sense of occasion prompted him to defer to Tansy. "Ladies first."

The boy seemed to see Tansy for the first time and mumbled in embarrassment, "The soup's lentil."

Tansy gave him a redeeming smile. "That suits me fine."

"I can recommend the steak pie." Eoin saw that Tansy looked doubtful. "They do an excellent ploughman's."

The boy hovered. Tansy chose the latter and watched as he wrote laboriously on his notepad.

"And a sparkling water." Then she turned her attention to Eoin. If he had looked out of place on the jetty he looked eminently at home in these surroundings.

Eoin began, "Craig told me that you are following up the story on the Tynwald art tax. You're quick off the mark!"

Tansy was prepared to admit that she did not have many writing contracts when Eoin added, "The enthusiasm of youth. I applaud you. It's quite a trek getting here from your part of the world. That's probably why I have never been. After I've crossed on the ferry I've had enough, and rarely venture past Liverpool."

"I came from Heynsham."

"Of course. Sensible route although fewer ferries. What can I tell you?"

"How will the Act work and how will it affect people, especially those who possess valuable old paintings?"

Their soup arrived with generous chunks of seeded brown bread on the side. The lad remained dumbstruck. Tansy with her blond hair, simple summer dress and high strapped sandals was remarkable by any standards, but the incongruity of Eoin with such a stunning girl seemed to amuse her companion. "I don't usually have company when I come here! Certainly not young journalists anyway!"

Tansy grinned. "That'll set them talking!"

"But to your question. It will work like this. I have liaised with the income tax office and secured a licence to verify the date of paintings, as best I can. The painting then has a barcode attached to it. Records are kept, by myself and by the office. Any transaction, and the barcode helps to track the painting."

Eoin looked at Tansy over his spectacles. "The island needed ways of increasing its income. Their coffers are desperately low and any hare-brained scheme was considered."

"Possibly not so outlandish after all?" Tansy eyed Eoin who gave her a satisfied grin.

"This will be a nice little earner for me," he admitted.

Tansy was not drawn in. "What about the owners?"

"Their reaction varies. Of the artists living on the island

there is widespread optimism. And so there should be as you will see when I show you my shop. Antiques are my main source of income but I sold all the paintings that I owned and now have a display wall of local artists."

"You sold all your paintings?"

"But I've bought a selection of contemporary paintings. It's a gamble but I might have a future Picasso among them."

Tansy thought for a moment. "I understand. You sold before the Act was made law, presumably on the mainland?" Eoin raised his eyebrows in acknowledgement. "How did you know to do that?"

"Because it all started during a discussion in my shop over a year ago. But I'll explain the rest later. And I've invited someone to meet you."

Eoin signalled across the room for the bill, and then he and Tansy walked further up the street to his antique shop. While Eoin unlocked the door, Tansy took a mental note of the exterior and the display window in case she needed the details for her piece.

"Phillip Glentenmont is due any minute." Eoin bustled around pulling out chairs, replacing some ceramics that he had left on his desk, and straightening one or two paintings that had tilted on their hooks. "He's the owner of Manquill Castle. The castle has been in the family for hundreds of years and he wanted to pick my brains regarding his collection of paintings. Most will be worthless now, I'm afraid. I suggested he come and meet you and he jumped at the chance."

"To meet me?"

"So that you can let people know what is happening here. Craig was right when he suggested that you are probably the front runner. Once the word is out we will be inundated by the press."

"You think so?" Tansy was doubtful. Eoin realised that Tansy underestimated the news industry and he feared the consequences. She was naïve if she thought that a story such as this would not provoke a spirited reaction, especially from journalists frustrated at missing this scoop.

"I know so! Stick with your magazine is my advice!"

The door creaked and a shaft of light silhouetted their visitor. Phillip was tall and athletic in build, in his late twenties, wearing jeans, a checked shirt and tan leather boots. He stood just inside the door for a moment.

"Come in! Phillip! This is Tansy Witt." Tansy enjoyed his look of admiration, and was pleasantly surprised that the owner of a castle was not the elderly tweed and corduroy military type that she had envisaged.

Although Eoin had provided chairs, they remained on their feet, and as an introduction Eoin showed them a few of his most treasured pieces before directing attention to the wall of paintings.

"All modern. A contrast to the rest of your collection," Phillip observed. "I take it that you sold before the crash. Shrewd move!"

"Do you have many paintings?" Tansy asked Phillip.

Phillip looked across at Eoin, who tipped his head on one side and answered for him. "Phillip's family have quite a collection, I'm afraid. Some were very valuable."

Tansy was curious. Phillip did not appear particularly upset. She was wondering how to broach the subject when Phillip said, "They've been in the family for years. I feel that I am the guardian for the next generation, just as my parents were for mine. Not just the castle and its contents but the farms and the estate."

"Can I ask you," Tansy began tentatively, "what your reaction is to this new law?"

"I heard that you were a journalist and expected some

question along those lines, so I've been thinking. Can we sit?"

Tansy produced her notepad. "Can I?"

"Of course. This is my opinion for what it is worth. If I needed to borrow money, for example to repair a roof, farm profits do not stretch to that sort of capital outlay, and I could have used the paintings as collateral. Now I can't. On the other hand my insurance bill, which was huge, will now be negligible, which is a bonus."

"But what about the massive loss in their value?" Tansy persisted.

Phillip smiled as if he had anticipated this aspect of her interview. "I would never sell them. They are part of what I inherited, they are part of Manquill Castle. Only if I were in dire straits would they be sold."

"But that option is now gone!" Tansy reiterated.

"They could just as easily go up in flames. We can't bank on anything."

Tansy could not fathom Phillip's almost debonair attitude to an event that she had presumed was catastrophic for people like him.

"In a way it's liberating!" Phillip announced.

Tansy's pen remained poised and Eoin sat forward in his chair. "How do you mean?"

"What time is your ferry?" Phillip asked suddenly. Tansy had temporarily forgotten that her time was limited.

Eoin looked perturbed. "You probably should be heading for the dock; they board thirty minutes before sailing."

"Could I contact you in the week if I need to, now that I have met you?" Tansy addressed both Eoin and Phillip.

"No problem. I'll help in any way I can," Eoin replied.

"I'll walk you to the ferry," Phillip offered.

Eoin gave him a knowing look. "That would be grand. Tansy, my dear, put our little island on the artistic map!"

"I will," Tansy answered. "I'll come back one day."

"So you will. You must." Eoin's enthusiasm was genuine.

Phillip closed the door behind them and they strode briskly towards the harbour. Tansy kept pace.

"How do you explain liberated?" Tansy asked breathlessly.

"So many new avenues open up now. I can spend the money that I usually spend on insurance on new paintings. I can have open days and create an income. I can rent them out for exhibitions, or lend them to our national gallery. The options are boundless. Without the weighty stone around my neck of worrying about all that money, untouchable by me, hanging on the walls causing envy and costing me a fortune just for being there, I can make plans, enjoy sharing, and revel in the fact that a burden has been lifted from my shoulders."

Tansy looked at Phillip's face as he finished. It was animated and boyish and Tansy began to laugh. "I'm so glad!" she explained, "I feared it would be an almighty blow for you."

"Don't get me wrong, for some people, people whose livelihoods revolve around dealing in paintings, it probably is."

"What you have told me is illuminating," Tansy said as she and Phillip reached the harbour and walked towards the queue that had formed to board the boat.

As Tansy searched in her bag for her ticket, Phillip said, "I forgot to ask. Who do you write for?"

"Not any magazine you'll have heard of. *Inside and Out.*"

"I'll make a point of finding it," Phillip asserted. "You'd better go, you don't want to be stranded here overnight!"

Tansy wondered if that were true. She felt a reluctance to leave. Phillip looked at her for a few seconds longer than

she expected before he shook her hand. "*Bannaght Lhiat!*
Farewell!"

Tansy joined the fast-moving queue and made a con-
scious decision not to turn and look back.

SEVENTEEN

It was the evening of the last day of the music festival when the Willow Man, a structure twenty feet high which had towered over the events for three days, was set alight. The outrageously large bonfire, which had been created over the previous weeks by anyone wishing to offload unwanted inflammable junk, was set in the centre of a field adjacent to where four marquees had been erected. Each marquee hosted a different genre of music and this variety was the reason for the success of the festival. There were bands for the young, family-friendly bands, local bands and in the main marquee, which was twice the size of the others, the headline bands.

Sunday night was the culmination of the weekend, when the very best of the best took to the stage in the main marquee and the best of the local bands took to their stage in a smaller marquee.

Tansy's experience over the weekend of the Willow Man festival so far had been enjoyable. The venue was spacious, the tents in the camping ground were not pitched cheek by jowl and neighbouring campers were considerate. The isolated location, with the hills and the loch as a backdrop, was as near to a rural escape as could be achieved when access to roads and amenities were accounted for.

The group had secured a good position from which to see the bonfire and as it was important to be vigilant or it would be quickly usurped, Tansy offered to guard their pitch while her friends fetched beer and lemonade from the bar. She watched the diverse crowd find their places for the finale. Young children played tig, couples strolled aimlessly, and a two-year-old in its all-in-one suit, whose plastic soles were already drenched with dew, padded by alone and unconcerned.

Yet Tansy felt empty. As a group they had linked up with others throughout the weekend, but whereas Reuben, David and Abigail appeared to know everyone, having been to school with many of them, Tansy had no such connection. They did not intend to exclude her, in fact their friends had actively sought her out to converse or to dance, but she still felt that they were making an effort because she was with Reuben.

The wait was longer than she expected. Reuben must have discovered another acquaintance or he certainly would have returned, even if it meant leaving David and Abigail at the bar. When Reuben, with his half-finished beer in one hand, while carefully balancing her lemonade in the other, steered his way towards her he reported gaily, "Fresh lemons and fresh mint! The mint is growing in pots right on the counter!"

"Trust you to notice that," Tansy laughed. "Who did you see?"

"Sorry, was I ages? Just another school friend. She and I both read business studies but she went to Newcastle. She was equally glad to be shot of uni at the end."

"I know the feeling," Tansy said placatingly, burying a moment of jealousy. As Reuben recounted the coincidences in his and the other girl's career paths, Tansy was aware that, if anything about that relationship was hidden, she too was concealing a secret that in normal circumstances she would not have withheld. It was uncomfortable, not being able to tell Reuben that she had a story which might be printed in a national newspaper, perhaps on that very day. She did not want to tell him in case her story was not accepted and then she would look foolish. It was one thing to write for a women's magazine, about which Reuben had long ago lost interest, but quite another to be treated as a bona fide journalist. If her story was printed she wanted to have the paper in her hand and show it to Reuben herself. It was frustrating, knowing that she would have to wait until the following morning, to see if she was in print, and then to have to wait until the evening before she could show Reuben.

"Say that again," Tansy apologised.

"I said that if Abi and David don't hurry they'll miss the lighting of the bonfire. I don't know what they hide amongst the wood, bales of hay probably, but it catches alight almost instantaneously."

Abigail and David made their way towards them, surrounded by a crowd of friends. "Can we join you?" one girl asked. Tansy wondered if she was the business studies student but decided she would rather not know.

The flames began, and faster and faster they flickered and leapt, thrusting their way upwards, drawn by the mighty legs of the willow giant. The heat intensified and those nearest the fire moved backwards. Tansy and her group stood up so as to have a better view and Reuben put his arm around her. She leant against him and rested her head on his shoulder, feeling as if this experience was uniquely for them.

"This has been a wonderful weekend," Reuben said beneath the raging crackles and sounds of spitting wood.

Suddenly he felt Tansy's body stiffen. Fireworks shot rockets and shooting stars high above. The Willow Man fell into the roaring flames. The increasing decibels smothered any reply Tansy attempted to make. Just as the fireworks reached a crescendo, the floodlights and stage lights were illuminated, and the long-awaited top-billing band crashed into their opening chords.

***

Early the next morning, having packed up their camp, Reuben drove to his parents' house alone. He had taken the day off work and so was spared another boring day in the office. He understood that it was necessary to endure a couple of years on the bottom rung before expecting to seek, or be sought out for, promotion. If he could be certain that a career juggling money with the resultant steady increase in salary was what he wanted, he would stick it, but he feared that too many of his father's doctrines had penetrated his skin, despite the inherited genes from his grandfather. His grandfather had shown hard graft and business acumen to become a wealthy grocer, and Reuben was not sure that it wasn't a more honourable way to earn a living than by dealing in paper money. On reflection it was not even paper money, just numbers flying through the ether with little tangible that Reuben could show for it. Perhaps further up the chain, where books had to balance, pounds and pence signs really did correlate with real notes and coins, there might be some satisfaction.

Reuben had seen an advertisement for a post in Dubai to manage excursions for tourists at one of the prestigious resorts. There was on-site training and Reuben did not think it was beyond his capabilities. It was the start of his search for something more adventurous, but he wanted to discuss his ideas, and warn his parents about his change of direction, before landing them with a fait accompli.

"We were not expecting you, Reuben," Deborah said

cheerfully. "You're probably wanting a bath!"

"That would be good. Do I stink? There were showers at the campsite but by this morning they were a mess and besides, the queue was huge."

"Have a coffee first?" Reuben nodded. "Was it a good weekend?"

"Excellent. Met a lot of my old pals. Anything happened here?"

"Florrie's working. She's not a schoolgirl any more."

"She has a job? Where?"

"At the bakers. The one with a café. Matty can't wait to start but she has to be sixteen."

Deborah handed Reuben a mug, poured a coffee for herself and joined him at the table. "Are you here for any other reason? Other than a bath?"

Reuben grinned. "Mother's intuition! I do want to ask your opinion on something."

"Jacob's in the garden."

"Has Dad done any more paintings?"

"You can see for yourself later. And help yourself to vegetables."

Reuben drained his mug and moved off towards the stairs. A few moments later Matty appeared and saw Reuben's bag.

"Reuben's here? Where? Why didn't you tell me?"

"Slow down Matty! By the time you've had breakfast Reuben should be down. He's been camping all weekend and has probably not been near a shower since Friday."

"Boys are Neanderthals."

"You mean that they don't spend hours with hair straighteners and makeup. I call it going back to nature."

Matty pulled a face and while Deborah washed lettuces and scrubbed potatoes she helped herself to toast and marmalade.

Jacob scuffed his boots one against the other as he removed them in the scullery.

"Dad, Reuben's here," Matty informed him excitedly.

"Trouble?"

"Not really. More like itchy feet," Reuben said as he descended the stairs.

"So that's how the land lies," Jacob observed. "That's not a bad thing."

"There's more to the world than this corner of Scotland," Deborah commented in support. "So where? More finance?" She handed him a plate of bacon and eggs.

"What's going on?" Matty interrupted, looking upset. "Where are you going?"

"I am looking at a different sort of job, in Dubai."

"Dubai?" Jacob was surprised. "They say that there's a sort of beauty to a desert."

"I've heard of Dubai," Matty said eagerly. "Isn't that where people earn loads of money?"

"Some do," Reuben laughed.

"I'd rather imagine you in Malaysia or India, or somewhere lush and beautiful," Deborah said wistfully.

"But you wouldn't mind? Even if I just managed a tourist enterprise?" Reuben began to sense their approval.

"We wouldn't come and visit."

Reuben knew his parents would neither want nor could afford to travel to Dubai. "I'll come back regularly."

Matty walked over to the window and turned her back on them. Reuben guessed that she was upset. "I'd have to keep an eye on you, wouldn't I, Matty?"

"Would you come back specially to see me?"

"Of course! You could even come out and visit."

Deborah went over to Matty and gently brought her back to the table. "That seems to be decided then, doesn't it? I am sure you will do very well out there."

"I'm glad you're here," Jacob said unexpectedly. "A friend of Andrew's is due to arrive. He's interested in my paintings. It might be handy if you came along."

"Perhaps he's the distributor of the little red dots?"

"He could be. His name is Craig."

When Craig arrived Jacob and Reuben took him directly to the mill. Reuben was accustomed to deciphering his father's paintings, but he wondered what Craig would make of them.

Craig walked around looking at the paintings for some while in silence and then joined Jacob and Reuben, who stood in front of one of the larger canvasses. On first sight it was obvious that there were two figures, but they were so ephemeral as regards to detail, yet made up of such substantial blocks of colour that the viewer was confused. Slowly the background emerged; a section of a painting hanging on a wall with the suggestion of a seascape; some curtains framing a window. Then it was possible to decipher that the two figures were sitting on a russet-coloured sofa and looking towards the window, the light suffusing their faces. One figure was tall and upright, sitting with her knees drawn up in a position only seen adopted by the young. Beside her, for both figures were unmistakably female, the other woman was older and sat hunched as if hugging her stomach. Both figures appeared to be pensive, perhaps sharing a thought. It might have depicted Florrie and her mother, but if it did then only those who knew them intimately would recognise their profiles.

Jacob led Craig around his studio uncovering further paintings until they returned to stand alongside each other by the original canvas.

Finally Craig spoke, quietly, as if amazed by his own reaction. "I can almost imagine what they are feeling!" Then abruptly he changed. "How many will you sell?"

Reuben wondered why Craig was interested in his father's work when Jacob had sold none for years and from his father's face he could see that he was equally puzzled. Instinctively he doubted whether Craig was sincere in his offer and feared that the price would be insulting. "Why would you do that?"

"I am specialising in contemporary paintings and I want to start with a splash. I gather that, apart from Taylor's little gallery, you have not exhibited recently. You can name your price. I'll tell you if it is unreasonable."

Reuben listened with concern, unable to stifle his urge to protect his father. To his relief Jacob hesitated.

"This has taken me a bit by surprise, but these paintings can't sit here for ever gathering dust. Can I let you know in a day or two?"

"A day or two is about my maximum. Here's my card."

Reuben smiled. His father only used a landline but Reuben decided that he would use the information to do some checks on his father's behalf. Nevertheless, a part of him was secretly elated, perhaps at last his father would be recognised for the artist that Reuben believed him to be. But would Craig understand that publicity was an anathema to Jacob and Deborah? He wondered how he might influence Craig in order to guard his parents' privacy while at the same time allowing him to promote their work.

After Craig had left, Reuben sensed that Jacob was prepared to trust him with his paintings. "You don't even need an hour, do you? You've already made up your mind."

EIGHTEEN

Andrew arrived at the college early that Monday morning. The building had been closed for a month and he wanted to check that the rooms that were to be used for the adult summer course were clean, and, more importantly, that the janitor had unlocked them. There were some janitors who guarded their long holiday jealously, but Andrew had a good rapport with his and it had not needed more than gentle persuasion to co-opt his help for the week. Fortunately the janitor was proud of the college, keen for Andrew to succeed, and was impressed that the teachers were prepared to give up a week of their holidays in order to run the course.

The response to their summer programme had gratified him. With so many art courses already established he was delighted that there appeared to be a place for one more and hoped that the reputation of McFarlane's was a draw. Moreover if the course went well, it would add to the college's growing reputation as a front runner in innovation.

Andrew opened the door to the studio and then rummaged around in the large cupboard for the easels. He planned to ask Gerald to meet the aspiring artists while he allocated them into groups with a tutor. He would then introduce himself and his staff, set out the programme for the week and leave them. He did not want to recreate a student environment, being aware that there might be some ex-art students amongst them who would be disappointed at not having their maturity acknowledged, and he wanted the course to develop its own style. There was still half an hour until it was due to begin but he expected both his staff and those attending to arrive early.

Callum was the first. He had, like Andrew, spruced up for the event and both wore jackets over neatly ironed shirts, and cotton trousers had replaced the usual jeans.

"Has anyone arrived yet?"

Callum must have known that he was the first, Andrew thought, which made his remark significant. "Can I help with anything?" Andrew spread out his hands to indicate that the place was ready.

"In that case I need a word with you. Did you see the papers at the weekend?"

"I glanced through. Anything in particular?"

Callum looked worried. "Probably not, but as someone in the group may have seen the article, I thought I should warn you."

Andrew was amused by Callum's conspiratorial manner. "A scandal?"

"Not a scandal, but it's a piece of news that might affect us. Tansy Witt wrote an article on undiscovered painters, and an astute reporter might track the story to here."

"Tansy Witt?"

"The reporter I spoke to after Taylor's exhibition for Jacob."

At that moment there were voices in the corridor. "Have you the article? Show me when we have everyone settled."

The adult summer school which was to commence that morning was an idea that Andrew had introduced and Gerald had to admit that it was an inspiration. The course was fully subscribed within ten days and they had been tempted to create a second week. Andrew, however, said that his staff needed their break and that it was good of them to give up their time, although they were hardly expected to commit without a fair remuneration. If it proved a success he could propose two sessions in the future. He planned to manage each day with one senior member of staff taking the lead.

Gerald had mixed feelings about the coming week. With Kerry so busy he did not mind giving up his time, and the money was always useful; it was the prospective clients that he dreaded. If only, like their students, they could be vetted. He had argued that to attract competent amateur artists they would somehow have to emulate the classier art courses that were already established and he urged Andrew to advertise carefully and not to under-price. Andrew heeded his advice. By the end of the first day Gerald would know whether it had worked. The worst scenario would be that he, and the others, limped through the week with a mixed bag of old codgers with fixed styles and implacable views; people who wanted to be told that a genius was lurking within which was only now being unleashed.

At the mid-morning break in the staff room only Gerald, Emily and Phyllis were present.

"Have you seen Andrew or Callum?" Gerald asked, hugging his restorative mug of coffee. The morning had been less daunting than he had feared but the habit was hard to break.

"In Andrew's office," Emily answered, unconcerned.

"Callum and Andrew haven't appeared all morning. Not once the group had settled in," Phyllis remarked. "They are cooking up something. You should know, Gerald."

Emily looked more interested now that there was a hint of gossip.

"Ever since the exhibition I have felt a change." Gerald was encouraged to continue by their obvious affinity with his mood. "Andrew never made any attempt to introduce you to Jacob. It could have been to spare him meeting too many people, but I wonder if he wants to perpetuate his myth. Since we are all senior members of staff I think it would have been courteous of him if he had, even if it was Taylor's exhibition. Who is this Taylor? Anyone know? The enigmatic owner of a gallery that just happens to be adjacent to the college, and just happens to open at the same time as Andrew launches all these projects."

"Could the one have facilitated the other?" Emily reasoned.

"It's logical," Phyllis agreed. "After all, Taylor is a friend of Andrew's and it would be to their mutual advantage, and to be fair, to our advantage, or do you suspect some underhand motive?"

"Another!" Gerald spluttered. "Another old friend. It's like the mafia. Was Taylor brought up here as well?"

"Not exactly. His wife was. She was the sister of one of their friends. That's probably why he bought the ware-house," Phyllis explained. "You see it all the time. Taylor also has an insurance business which he has relocated in town, did you not know?"

Gerald shook his head. There seemed to be too many convenient coincidences.

"So how do you explain," he paused for effect, "why someone bought all those pictures that night?"

"They did?" Phyllis sounded surprised. It was apparent that it was news to both her and Emily.

"Didn't you see the stickers? They weren't there before Andrew gave his speech and as most people left after that, only a few saw them."

"There was a piece in the paper yesterday," Phyllis said vaguely. "It was about an unknown artist. It could have been about Jacob, I suppose."

"If it was then we'll have newspaper reporters around here before we know it," Gerald said grimly. "The last thing any of us needs is that sort of publicity."

Phyllis placed a hand sympathetically on his arm. "I understand how fiercely proud you are of the college, but there is bound to be an explanation."

Towards the end of the break Callum and Andrew joined them. Emily commented reproachfully, "Our artists have been wondering where you were."

Andrew apologised. "Something came up. Nothing to do with the college. We'll make it up and let you off early."

As Gerald, Phyllis and Emily walked away from the college at the end of the afternoon. Emily said, "Well, we're none the wiser."

***

"Gerald. This is curious." As he walked through the door at the end of the day Kerry held up an envelope from the morning's post. "It's from an insurance firm. The address is an office in town. Do you know it?"

"I've not noticed one, but I'm not that surprised. I haven't been down the town recently. Is it in the main street?"

"At the far end near the Crown and Keys. There was a vacant shop there, I remember."

"What about the letter?" Gerald had his mind only half on Kerry's mail, the other half was attending to his own.

"It's setting a forecast for the market next year and suggesting some insurance scenarios. There's a section on insurance of art and ceramics which I presume includes sculpture. The letter suggests that there might be a focus on modern art in the near future and that I might want to consider re-evaluating my insurance policy."

"It's probably just a way to gain your custom," Gerald

commented. "If you are happy with your insurer why change?"

"That's my reaction. But it's still curious." Kerry decided to file the letter rather than bin it. There was something she had read recently which she thought had given the same message. Besides, if the insurer was in the town there was nothing to stop her calling in and enquiring when she had a free moment. If she ever had a free moment she thought, imagining such a luxury.

"Kerry. I might be imagining things, but something is going on at McFarlane's."

"What do you mean, something's going on?" Kerry asked sceptically. It was her opinion that the year had been a strangely successful one if her business was a reflection of a general upsurge in interest in the town and its facilities. Her shop had attracted an increase in visitors and it was not only, she was certain, because of a fresh coat of paint or an inspired window dressing. Her sales had been up and surprisingly her more pricey and adventurous purchases had been popular. The move by Andrew to enable the junior students to exhibit and sell items that now formed a part of her stock, had proved useful. Kerry discovered that the display of student work created an opening through which she could engage with her customers. There is a latent artist in most people, she assumed, and that personal contact often resulted in a sale.

"Let me explain," Gerald said. "It has been an experimental year. Andrew has been introducing some innovative ideas and I am sure that they all benefit the college, but I can't help feeling that there's more to it."

"How can that be? What do you think is happening?" Despite herself Kerry was intrigued. "Isn't it just that you have been encouraged to come up with ideas, like the one in the magazine I told you about?"

Gerald wondered if he was imagining it because he had felt side-lined recently. Callum had been given an increase in administrative work, work which he felt that he should have had as deputy, and he had been offered little by way of promotion to compensate, but when he told Kerry she assured him that it was because he was the better teacher. Even with her complimentary assessment of his talents, Gerald remained perturbed.

"Have we yesterday's paper?"

"What for? You'll find it in the usual place."

"Which is?"

"Beside the recycle bins," Kerry answered irritably.

When Kerry joined him in the kitchen Gerald apologised. He folded the newspaper so that the article he had been searching for was exposed. "Read this and tell me what you think. I'll pour you a glass of wine."

"White please, just a small one," Kerry recognised his gesture of conciliation. "Thanks."

The article was not long and Kerry had skimmed through it by the time Gerald returned with two glasses which were already forming condensation on the outside.

"It's by Tansy Witt," Kerry commented.

"Who is Tansy Witt? Should I know?"

"The young journalist at Taylor's exhibition. She came to see me the next day."

Gerald shook his head. "I don't remember her. I do remember you said that there was a girl who wrote for a glossy magazine."

"Same girl. She must have gone up a notch. But that's not the point. This painter she's writing about, it must be Jacob. What's all this about new laws and searching for new painters?"

"That's what I ask myself. I think Callum and Andrew know and plan to profit from it."

"Is that so bad?"

"It is if Andrew is using the college. The fact that he has said nothing to me makes me suspicious."

Kerry was cautious. "Aren't you reading too much into Andrew's silence? Perhaps he's said nothing because there is nothing to be said."

Gerald was riled. "I'm sure that my hunch is right. There has to be something going on. I mean to find out. I'll think it over this evening and find a way to check things out. Think, Kerry, if the college was involved in a scheme for personal gain, we'll all be out of a job."

"I don't see how you would be." Kerry attempted to calm him. "Andrew would never be foolish enough to compromise his job, and it isn't in Callum's nature. And if they were profiteering, it would be they who would be out of a job, and then you could take Andrew's place."

There seemed nothing to say after that since they both knew that Gerald aspired to the position of principal.

NINETEEN

As Craig drove away from viewing Jacob's paintings he had to swerve to avoid a car driving towards him in the narrow lane. He was under the impression that Jacob was somewhat reclusive and that visitors were rare but wondered if another dealer had anticipated the way that business was changing and was also hoping to persuade Jacob to sell. It seemed unlikely that the knowledge which he held was already being disseminated. It was only four weeks since Tynwald and only to Tansy Witt, he believed, would Eoin have told this exclusive piece of news. It did not occur to him that Tansy, who was a writer for a fashion magazine, might have decided after all to write a piece for a major newspaper.

However, Craig was elated and his mind was only partially concentrating on the road as he processed the impact of Jacob's extraordinary personality. No one could fail to be affected by the strength of his dedication to his art. In the studio Craig was aware of an insight into the working of an artist's mind that even he had not previously experienced. While attempting to analyse this new sensation he could feel the adrenalin churning through his body and his thoughts taking off into the realms of conjecture. It was a long time since he had taken such a gamble. The excitement of the hunt for a potentially winning deal was a distant memory but now the thrill returned. He felt the need to confide in someone and almost unconsciously headed into the town in search of John.

"Come in. What news? You've been to see Jacob?" John was outside in the garden, wheelbarrow and fork were being put to good use judging by the mound of couch grass and buttercups.

"I have offered for all of them. As many as he wants to sell. Only just in time, I think. I met another car heading up his lane."

"Another dealer?" John was doubtful.

"Possibly. I can't rule it out."

John was, however, incredulous. "Jacob has sold? I won't ask what you offered. I can't begin to imagine what they might be worth."

"Reuben was there. He was more cagey. I think he's trying to protect his father and make sure he is not cheated. Which is fair enough. I've given them a couple of days."

"What if they don't come back to you?"

"Then I know that they won't sell to anyone. I'll leave it and try again later in the year. It would suit me because I'd have more idea where the market is going. I am reasonably certain that if Jacob does decide to sell, he will sell to me."

"I hope for your sake that that's the case. You've plenty of credentials and I expect people feel a loyalty to their original contact. All the more so in Jacob's case since no dealer has approached him in years."

Craig took the observation with a wry smile. "You realise that I am relying solely on intuition here."

***

In his studio Jacob surveyed the stacks of paintings that were laid against the walls and watched as Reuben selected one canvas from its pile, set it aside, and then selected another.

"You seem to have arranged them in some sort of chronological order," Reuben observed. He had grown up watching the paintings develop, had taken them for granted, but now he viewed them from a new perspective. "I can remember that one from when I was starting school." The painting was predominantly yellow and blue, and Jacob had been experimenting with a quasi-bas-relief, cutting into woodchip to enhance the effect. Reuben remembered a day on the beach, and then coming home and finding that his father had recreated it in his studio.

"Those later ones, when I was at secondary school, were more difficult to decipher, but I can see how you were developing now. The colours themselves don't matter, just the relationships between them."

He lifted a painting. The scene could have been a headland at sunset in pinks and greys, but Reuben was not prepared to articulate this. "I really like this one." He glanced at his father whose face was inscrutable. "Are you going to sell?"

"They can't sit here for ever."

Reuben put the painting down. "Then we had better get started. Craig said that he needed to know within two days. How do you want to do it?"

Jacob crossed his arms, raised his shoulders and then let them slump. "I have no idea. What do you suggest?"

Reuben pointed to the stacks of canvasses. "We should hedge our bets. Your bets really. Divide each pile into two and offer to sell Craig half. Then price them. We could suggest to Craig that he can buy the rest at the same sort of prices, or we could ask for more, if the first batch sells."

Jacob seemed to be prepared to accept whatever Reuben suggested. "So start with the early ones?"

They worked steadily through the afternoon, punctuated by visits from Deborah with tea and homemade cake. She hung around longer at each visit, saddened to think of the paintings, as familiar to her as her children and indivisible from her feelings for Jacob, disappearing from her life.

Florrie and Matty came to watch the proceedings but when they began to add their opinions to the decision making, Reuben told them firmly to return to the house. He told them that they could come at the end and would be able to veto two pictures. Florrie disliked Reuben's superior behaviour but Matty, once she understood the veto system, relished her anticipated show of power.

The family waited for Abigail to return from work before they sat down to eat. She was late and when she did arrive she pushed open the door, almost falling through it as she did so, slammed it shut and leant her back against it. "There are cars and vans all down the lane! People with cameras, groups of them, one man was on top of his Jeep. They asked me if I was your daughter, Dad, and if they could interview me. What is happening?"

At that moment the telephone rang. Deborah picked up the receiver and almost immediately returned it to its stand. "That's the *Morning Star*. He said he was a reporter. Why?"

"It must be Craig, or something to do with Craig," Reuben deduced. "No one answer the telephone. Let's eat and then I'll try and find out what is going on."

Deborah removed their meal from the oven while the family sat silently. Reuben waited for a comment from Jacob but none was forthcoming.

Eventually Deborah asked, "How many cars, Abi?"

"Seven or eight. They looked set for the night. They were very polite but I really did have nothing to tell them. It's okay, Dad. I didn't say who I was."

Jacob turned to Reuben. "Why should Craig's visit spark a media interest unless he's told them something? Told them something that we don't know."

"But what?" asked Deborah, mildly shaken, but in disbelief. "Why should anything we do be of any interest to anybody?"

Matty left the table to look out of the window. The sky was darkening. "I can see car headlights, and I think they have spotlights." She quickly drew the curtain across the window.

"They have probably confused us with some celebrity," Florrie suggested.

Reuben finished his last mouthful and pushed his plate to one side. "Shall I ring Craig?"

"Why would he pretend to buy your paintings and then alert the media?" Deborah asked reasonably. "Reuben, give him a call, it's all we can do in the first instance." She looked enquiringly towards Jacob, who gave no sign that he disagreed.

As Reuben left the room Jacob said, "It's our only course of action. Craig is the only person who might have an explanation. No one else has been here and he might have an answer. It's a pity, because I trusted him and I am not usually wrong with my judgements."

Reuben returned from the adjacent room. "I've left a message to call us. I didn't say why. He'll probably think it's about the sale. Shall I go and speak to the reporters?"

"You might as well," Jacob said, and then changed his mind. "Give it half an hour for Craig to answer."

Deborah and Abigail cleared supper and disappeared into the scullery. Jacob and Reuben sat in the living room on either side of the telephone.

Florrie was about to leave the kitchen when Matty held her back. "Florrie, we're going to spy on them," Matty announced, "they're spying on us." Florrie was not sure whether to stay with Jacob or be caught up in the web of Matty's fantasy. As her father had been almost mono-syllabic, the fabrications of Matty's imagination seemed preferable. She followed Matty up the stairs and they peered out from the landing window.

"What if we are famous and we don't know it?" Matty whispered to Florrie.

"Who famous?" Florrie said disparagingly. She was, after all, the older sister. "Not you, anyway."

"Could be Reuben. He might have saved someone's life in Glasgow and never told us."

"Don't be stupid, Matty. The only person who could be famous in our family is Dad. It hasn't happened yet so it's not likely to happen now."

"But what if he was," Matty persisted. Florrie could see that Matty equated famous with rich and was creating a new and fanciful life for herself.

"We'd hate it," Florrie said damningly.

Downstairs, beside Reuben, the telephone rang and he lifted the receiver but did not speak. "That newspaper again!" he told Jacob. "I'll ring Craig and ask him to let the phone ring four times and then we'll ring him back."

Once he had done so Jacob said, "This is ridiculous."

"It certainly is," Deborah said as she joined them. "I think Reuben should go and speak to the reporters." Reuben stood up, ready to go out and confront them when the phone rang. He signalled to Deborah to allow it to ring. "Four rings. That's Craig."

Sensing that her mother was feeling anxious, Abigail moved to sit beside her. Reuben observed her action and was grateful that, now that she was living at home, she could help him to support their parents. Abigail felt more curious than upset by the congregation of cars outside in their lane, but like him she objected to the intrusion on their privacy. Reuben picked up the receiver.

"Craig, Reuben here. No, it's not about the paintings. We did a lot of sorting this afternoon, and chose the ones for sale." Reuben was unable to continue while he listened to Craig's reply. Jacob looked questioningly, but Reuben shook his head and then interrupted Craig as he was speaking. "It's about the reporters. The lane is full of them." He paused to allow Craig to comment. "You have no idea? They asked Abi if she was Jacob's daughter." There was silence until eventually Reuben said. "That would be good of you. See you tomorrow." He replaced the receiver. Matty and Florrie stood in the doorway, and Abigail warned them with a look to keep silent.

Reuben turned to his parents. "Craig will be here as early as he can in the morning. I must go back to Glasgow. You'll be all right once he's here. Mum? He honestly did not know what it could be about. He promises that he has not spoken about us to anyone."

TWENTY

Early the next morning, before the summer art class was due to begin, Gerald walked along the street in the direction of Lauren's office. He had decided to consult her and although he did not know her, many of his acquaintances did, and vouched for her approachability. More importantly, for Gerald, she was a local woman who would know, or could find out, any current gossip that might explain the newspaper article. Gerald did not intend to tell Lauren his reason for contacting her because he felt that if his suspicions were proved unfounded, he would be considered a time waster. He feared that if he was seeing conspiracies where there were none Lauren could, rightly, blame him for over-reacting. However, she had local contacts and would be able to verify the story. Never had he felt such an outsider.

When Gerald reached the office he pushed open the door and the young lad sitting at a desk asked him to take a seat while he informed Lauren of his arrival. The office had two desks, with the obligatory computer and telephone, a few chairs along the wall beside the door, and in the space between the desks was a sturdy filing cabinet and a large printer. On the walls hung two calendars donated by local garages, both turned to the correct month, some family photos over one desk and two watercolours above the other. Gerald's eye was drawn to the watercolours. It was second nature for him to look critically at paintings, and he was pleasantly surprised. They were local scenes that he knew well but the style was unusual and he wondered where he might have seen it before.

David came through the door.

"Who is the artist? It's not signed," Gerald asked.

"Abi. My girlfriend. She used to be at the college."

"Not one of my students. They're good."

"Thanks." David waited awkwardly. "Mrs McGill is free now."

Lauren left her seat to greet Gerald and shake his hand. "Sorry to keep you. How can I help?"

"I'm vice principal at McFarlane's. You may know my wife, Kerry, who owns the art gallery."

"I recognise you. From the exhibition," she said warmly. "We did not have a chance to speak. There was such a crowd."

Gerald was not sure how to begin. He brought the newspaper cutting from his jacket pocket. "Have you seen this? I am wondering if you know anything. You see, I am concerned that it might impact on the college."

While Lauren read, Gerald sat in the chair on the opposite side of her desk and looked around. Her office was unexpectedly austere, with an out-sized desk which was plain and functional and bare walls except for a chart of events. In one corner was a sink with upturned coffee mugs, a kettle and a fridge. He was not sure what he expected, but it was not this spartan environment. In some ways he found it reassuring, because it implied that Lauren was there to work. He sat back, at least the chairs were well upholstered, and waited for her response.

"There are no murmurings of a law in Scotland." She was about to type on her computer when Gerald interrupted her.

"There is on the Isle of Man, if that is what you are searching."

"I can't see how it affects us here." Lauren was silent. "I will have to think about it. Why are you worried for your college?"

Gerald was not sure how to articulate his presentiment that there was more to the story than appeared on the surface. "It couldn't happen here?" he countered.

Lauren's smile wrinkled her face. "Unlikely. If it did how might it affect McFarlane's College?"

"It might explain some of the changes in practice. To be honest, it's conjecture. I'd be grateful if you would contact me if you do uncover something." Gerald stood up to leave, convinced that his interview had made no sense; Lauren, though, knew not to dismiss anything, however bizarre it appeared on the surface, and to keep an open mind.

"I'll keep my ear to the ground, I assure you," Lauren endeavoured to put Gerald at his ease. "And please feel free to contact me again."

Gerald closed the office door, and gave David a wave of acknowledgement on his way out. It was only a few moments later that Lauren remembered what had been niggling her at the mention of the Isle of Man.

"David!" Lauren was speaking before she had fully entered the room. "Sorry," she said when she saw that David was engrossed on his screen. "Can you spare a minute?"

David looked up. "I was making a search on behalf of your little OAP," he explained, referring to their current case.

"Thanks. This is about the Tynwald. Can you remember what you read regarding the Art Act?"

David nodded. "It wasn't so much what I read, but what

my Dad told me. He said that they are going to confiscate, or ban the sale of, all paintings that are over a hundred years old. It seemed weird to me."

"It now makes sense to me." Lauren sat on the spare chair beside David's desk. David shuffled through a pile of correspondence, prioritising them and wondering if it was a good time to ask Lauren's opinion on one of them, when suddenly she tapped her hand several times repeatedly on his desk.

"I've got it," she said. "It's clever. Think about it. It could, I am only saying that it could, become law here."

David looked puzzled.

"As a way of making money, and scuppering tax havens and tax avoidance."

David had the slimmest understanding of finance. He was not yet in a position to pay tax but he was aware that some companies had methods to evade paying.

"There is so much money locked up in a piece of canvas," Lauren commented. David wanted to know why Lauren had initiated the discussion, but due to the delicate balance of confidentiality, he was hesitant to ask.

"The client who has just left, he's from the art college. He thinks that something is rumbling already, but I can't see how." Lauren laid the newspaper cutting on his desk. "He left this article, you might like to read it."

***

Craig arrived at Jacob's house, as promised, early. Reuben and Abi had already left but Florrie and Matty were having breakfast when he knocked on the door. Jacob ushered him into the kitchen where Deborah was waiting. "Thank you for coming."

"I could not ring. Reuben explained that, sensibly, you

are not answering any calls. The reporters are still camped out in the lane. I had to walk from the road. Have you spoken to them?"

"We waited for you. We hoped that you might have discovered something." Jacob took him through to the living room.

"I'm in the dark as much as you," Craig responded. However, he had one possible explanation, but it was more of a dealer's hunch than a logical deduction.

"What I think that I can explain is why your paintings might have a market where they did not before."

He stopped and Jacob invited him with a gesture to take a seat. Deborah and the girls quickly followed suit.

Craig chose his words. "It still does not explain the media interest." The family listened as Craig outlined their trip to the Isle of Man, and what he had discovered while he was there.

Jacob quickly understood the implications. "This affects your trade if that ruling is extended into Scottish law."

"Precisely," Craig affirmed. "It's a big 'if', but I am a gambler."

"You mean if it did become law here. That still does not explain the media, and us, and now," Deborah commented. "If you say that is all you know, you should go and ask those reporters."

While Craig was outside, Florrie and Matty pestered their parents with questions, which they were unable to answer. Eventually Craig returned. "Tansy has written in one of the Sunday papers, hinting at the changes in the law, and whetting people's appetites with the prospect of undiscovered geniuses. The article led with a story of a little-known artist residing in obscurity. It only took one reporter to trace the trail and discover the artist from the description in the article. The reference was to the exhibition that Taylor held. It was not long before other reporters followed like lemmings."

Jacob shook his head. "Is it such a big story?"

"The media can make something big if they set their minds to it." Craig could see how the story of a mysterious genius could create news in the middle of the silly season. In July and August reporters had to search for subjects. Craig suspected that one of their group might have spoken to a journalist but since he excluded John and Andrew from his equation it left Taylor or Callum. "Callum is working this week. If you agree I'll go and pick his brains. Failing that, I'll look out Taylor."

Craig had not expected the line of cars to trail him, but he was not perturbed since Jacob would be relieved that the reporters were no longer blocking his lane. He led the convoy to the entrance of the college and parked.

***

While the amateur artists took their mid-morning break Gerald wandered out for a breath of air and some respite from his intensely focused students, and as he exited into the forecourt he saw that a group of reporters had assembled on the perimeter of the car park. Gerald felt certain that their presence was the result of whatever had instigated Andrew and Callum's secretive behaviour. He decided to tackle Andrew immediately.

"Andrew." He opened the office door without knocking, and was discomforted to see that he was not only with Callum, but that they were both with a stranger. "Can I have a word with you?"

"Come in," Andrew invited.

"I'd rather speak out here," Gerald said aggressively. Andrew left the two men and closed the door of his office behind him. "What's going on?" Gerald demanded. "Why is the press outside? I think you owe me an explanation." Gerald had wound himself up into such a height of suppressed rage that he did not register Andrew's blank look.

"Do not deny that you are keeping something from me. You and Callum, and who knows who else of your cronies."

"Gerald, I know as little as you," Andrew began.

"How can you say that when you and Callum were in cahoots all yesterday?"

"Yesterday?" Andrew once again seemed surprised. "Callum told me that there had been an article in a Sunday paper which our mature students might be discussing."

Gerald's rage did not reduce and the quiet calm of Andrew's reply angered him further. Gerald wrenched open the door to the office. "Well perhaps your friends can enlighten me, or us," he added sarcastically. He directed his question to the stranger, "So why the press?" Craig was taken aback by a rudeness he had not encountered for some years.

"Everyone. Sit down," Andrew commanded as Craig got to his feet. "Gerald, this is Craig. He is here asking the same questions. Between him and Callum we may have some answers." Gerald had no option but to sit down.

"The press followed me here," Craig said, and then Callum took over.

"We have purposefully kept Andrew in ignorance of all of this."

Gerald barked, "All of what?"

Craig then said, "I'll start at the beginning. But even I don't know the full story."

Slowly, as Craig recounted their trip to the Isle of Man, the news that they had gleaned over a year ago, and the subsequent events, and as Gerald began to realise that

Andrew had been kept in the dark to protect his position, his aggression turned to curiosity.

Callum completed the picture. "So the article by this journalist on Sunday has ignited, based on conjecture, a search for a hidden artist. Unfortunately the writer naively gave enough clues for these reporters to trace Jacob, and, unwittingly, Taylor supplied the final clue. He told the reporter that he presumed that the artist they were searching for was the one whose work he had shown at his exhibition. He rang me as soon as he was off the phone, fearing that this might happen."

Gerald was now genuinely perplexed. "But isn't this an artist's dream, to be discovered?"

Andrew sighed. "For most of us, yes, but I very much doubt that Jacob will see it that way."

Craig decided, in order to fully support Andrew and convince Gerald that there had been no collusion, to tell them how he was involved. "Yesterday I told Jacob that I would buy all or as many of his pictures as he wanted to sell. Andrew had no knowledge of this. The press is here because of me. It's Jacob that they are interested in, not the college."

Gerald felt somewhat deflated. He had hurried to conclusions, even going so far as to involve Lauren, and now there was an explanation, albeit not a simple one. By the end of the day he would have to admit this to Lauren and to Kerry. In the meantime there was the spectre of the press camped outside his college and some over-curious amateur students who would need to know the reason why.

Gerald grabbed the moment to deflect from his over-zealous behaviour. "So what do the press want and who do we send out to speak to them?"

"It has to be Andrew, as principal," volunteered Callum. "He also knows the least."

"I'll come with you," Craig offered, and Gerald did not object. To placate Gerald and to help resolve his conflict with Andrew, he added, "now that I know why the press are here I need to inform Jacob and I assure you that the press will leave your forecourt and follow me. There will be no need for your painting group to be aware that they were here." He did not add that the group would probably hear about it eventually, but at least when they emerged from their day's session the car park would be clear.

As they headed out to meet the press Andrew asked Craig, "How much do we tell them?" Andrew took the article out of his shirt pocket. "Have you seen this, the article that sparked it all?" They spent a few minutes in the corridor while Craig absorbed the information and read it through to the end.

"Tansy Witt!" Craig said with a sigh. Andrew waited, wondering why he had read out the name of the journalist. "Oh dear!" Craig added, but he said nothing more and the two men made their way to face the barrage of questions that the reporters had ready for them.

TWENTY-ONE

When Gerald called back at Lauren's office David recognised him as the teacher who had looked so disturbed that morning. Gerald felt that it was only fair to Lauren to tell her what he had learnt that morning. "Is Lauren free? I only need a few moments."

Gerald was not long with Lauren who walked him to the door. "It was good of you to come by, Gerald, and I am glad that there is a simple reason for the reporters. I don't suppose this will be the end of it, once they have the scent of a story at least one will pursue it."

"So long as the story stays away from here," Gerald said firmly, but he smiled his thanks.

When she returned, David was midway through a conversation on the telephone.

"Has something happened?" Lauren asked when he had finished. David was embarrassed that she had seen his concern, yet he was so perturbed that he decided not to conceal the news.

"Abi rang to say that reporters have been camping around her house."

Lauren did not react as he expected. "That teacher tells me a dealer is sorting them out. They got wind of a story in a Sunday paper and tracked a mystery painter to his lair."

"You mean Jacob?" David looked shocked.

"I do. Hopefully it will soon blow over." Lauren appeared

to think that the matter was finished with and headed back to her desk.

David picked up the phone again, and dialled.

"We've had the press camping outside our house all night," David heard Abigail's outraged voice. "Someone called Craig who wants to buy Dad's paintings is helping but he said that he didn't know anything. Can you give me a lift home?"

"Is your Dad all right?"

"He appears calm but Mother is furious and said that it's cruel sending reporters to hound them and invade their privacy."

"I'll ask if I can leave now and I'll pick you up. Perhaps this Craig will provide an answer."

David drove to the café where Abigail was waiting. "They have given me the rest of the day off!" she said breathlessly, climbing into the car and closing the door.

They had time to exchange their accounts of events and for David to reveal that the reporters had also been to the college but he did not feel justified in divulging that one of the tutors had been upset to the extent that he had called on Lauren. As David and Abigail approached the house the lane was clear, but a stranger's car was parked outside the house.

When they entered the kitchen Deborah and Jacob were sitting with a third person who Jacob introduced as Craig. On the table between them was a newspaper cutting. All three looked up, wearily in the case of Deborah and Jacob, and nervously in the case of Craig.

Deborah invited them to sit. "There's a pot of tea, it's still warm, and help yourselves to some cake." She appeared agitated.

"What's up, Mum? The reporters have gone," Abigail said as she pulled her chair up beside her mother. David sat beside Jacob. They looked from face to face and waited for Jacob to speak.

"Craig can tell you," he said. "Do you mind?"

Craig picked the piece of paper up from the table and David recognised the cutting that Lauren had shown him, as he handed it to them to read. "Andrew, the principal, gave this to me earlier today."

***

Reuben, as he arrived at his Glasgow flat, heard the telephone ringing. How had he forgotten Tansy? She would have been worried at being unable to reach him.

"Reuben." Tansy's voice was excited. "Where have you been? I have been trying to reach you to tell you that I had an article printed in a Sunday newspaper," Tansy rushed on. "When I got back here from the festival, my flatmate had kept the paper. Isn't it amazing? Why aren't you saying anything and why weren't you answering last night?"

Reuben tried to concentrate. It was only a day ago that they had left the festival, sorted through the paintings, and that the reporters had arrived.

"It was weird," he tried to explain. "Our house was surrounded by reporters and when they kept ringing we stopped answering the phone."

"That explains why. Shall we meet later? You can tell me more about the reporters. See you at the usual place." Tansy rang off. Reuben stared at his phone and wondered if either of them had listened to the other during their conversation.

The feeling of unease that Reuben had had all day persisted as he travelled the short distance to meet Tansy. He wondered why she had not been more shocked by his mention of reporters. Perhaps because in her line of work this happened routinely, but she had not reacted as he had expected.

Reuben was already seated when Tansy arrived. She looked particularly beautiful because the last time that they had been together both of them had felt groggy, looked dishevelled and were uncomfortably unwashed. Reuben's misgivings regarding her calm acceptance of his news receded as he watched her walk towards him, her shoulder bag swinging in time with her hips, making her way between the tables. Recently her hair had been cut in a bob and she was wearing a figure-hugging white t-shirt and a pair of denim shorts. He enjoyed the undisguised looks of admiration that she evoked from the men at the adjacent table.

"It seems ages since I've seen you!" Tansy kissed Reuben and began to speak before he could answer. "I wondered why you didn't answer the phone, but I so wanted to show you this." She fumbled with the zip of her bag and then brought out a newspaper cutting. "This is it. This is my article in the Sunday paper." She held it out happily and then moved her chair so that she could watch the expression on his face.

Reuben took a long time to read the article and Tansy fidgeted when she saw that he was reading it through for a second time.

"Tansy, what have you done?" The tone of Reuben's voice was measured but with a metallic edge.

"I don't know what you mean."

Reuben pointed to the cutting, and pushed it across the table towards her. "This, this is why our house is surrounded by reporters."

"I didn't think anyone would pick up on it, but I think you are right."

"Of course I'm right Tansy!" Reuben said angrily.

"'Mysterious painter who recently had an exhibition in a town renowned for its art.' It doesn't take much sleuth work to narrow it down."

"Why are you so cross?" Tansy asked.

Reuben stared at her uncomprehendingly. "Do you understand nothing, Tansy? There have been reporters camped around our house. I thought it was Craig's doing, but I believe him now when he said he knew nothing."

"Why Craig?" Tansy looked shaken and appeared to be clutching at straws.

"Craig is not relevant now," Reuben said irritably, "it's not to do with him. He wanted to buy some of father's paintings, that's all."

"But isn't that good?"

"Yes, it's good. Craig was not the one who galvanised a crowd of reporters to hound my father and monopolise the phone."

"So that's why you did not answer the phone?"

Reuben was exasperated. "Now you are getting the idea." He raised his voice and Tansy became overwhelmed with embarrassment.

"I thought," she said, "I thought, that you would be pleased."

When Reuben understood that Tansy was unable to grasp the situation and its impact on his father, he got up and, with no explanation, turned his back on her and walked away. Tansy sat immobile, her face pinched and lips pressed together, her hands clasped and head bowed, until Reuben returned with two glasses of beer.

He sat opposite her and then asked, "Let me get this straight. You thought that by writing an article on my father, without telling him, he would be happy?"

Tansy again spoke softly. "You always said that he was overlooked and underrated."

"But you did this without asking him?" Reuben remained outraged.

"It was my first attempt at writing for a national. I could not expect it to be printed. I only hoped." They sat without speaking.

Finally Reuben said, "At the worst it's a breach of confidence and at best it's naivety. I'll go for the latter." He was no more conciliatory.

Tansy summoned up her courage. "Your father?"

"He'll probably know why, by now Craig has probably found out about your article," he said flatly. "I don't know about Father's reaction but Mother will be upset."

Tears welling in her eyes, Tansy pushed her drink away, barely touched, and stood up. "I can only say that I am sorry." She picked up her bag and put the strap over her shoulder.

Reuben was implacable. "Where are you going?"

Tansy did not answer. Reuben did not watch her leave. He finished his beer and then hers, drinking quickly, and followed her. When he reached the pavement Tansy was almost out of sight. He hurried after her but then changed his mind and slowed to a walk.

He passed a stationery shop and on impulse decided to see what Tansy had written in the most recent issue of her magazine. He had not read any of her writing for months. He wandered along the racks of magazines. There were so many, and on so many subjects. One wall was dedicated to homes and interiors and these seemed the most promising shelves. Reuben had always hoped, for Tansy's sake, that *Inside and Out* was popular, it certainly had been at the outset when Tansy started working with them, but journals had a habit of disappearing overnight when their regular readers were attracted by a new publication.

Reuben followed the row of journals, moved a few aside

to see those that had become hidden, and then he saw it. It was unmistakable. On the front cover was Jacob's painting of the girl which they had seen resting at the top of the staircase in the mill. He picked up the magazine and, holding it out, he looked from left to right as if to ask a bystander what they thought. All ideas of reconciliation evaporated. Almost forgetting to pay, he strode out of the shop and without considering the distance, his mind churning, walked until he reached Tansy's flat. He pressed the buzzer. "Let me in, Tansy. We need to talk."

As soon as Tansy saw that month's publication of her magazine in Reuben's hand, her face lost its colour. She led the way into the sitting room and sat down.

Reuben remained standing. "How could you let this happen? What right do you have to use one of his paintings? Where did you get the photograph?" He towered over her. "Could you not stop your editor, after all that has happened?"

Tansy answered in a monotone, "I took the picture at the exhibition. I did ask the editor but she said that it was too late. Like I said before, I thought I could help."

Reuben walked up and down the short length of the room. Quietly Tansy began to cry.

"This is it, Tansy, you realise?" Reuben opened the magazine to the page of Tansy's piece. With huge sarcasm he quoted, "The mystery of the little red dots." He turned towards her. "A very fine story you have made. Every tourist will be searching for the secret location, not so secret as it turns out, of the unknown artist. None of them care about art, but they all love a celebrity. That's what you have turned my father into, Tansy, a celebrity." Tansy sat mute.

Reuben paced up and down a few times, and to emphasise his exasperation he said, "What do they do to celebrities?

They put them on a pedestal only to take it from under them when they have had enough. I do not want my father humiliated again. You can keep your magazine and you had better examine your career in journalism."

Tansy still did not speak, nor did she look at him. She remained seated, unmoving.

He turned towards the door and then, just as he was about to leave he added, "I meant to tell you earlier, but until today I had not made up my mind. I'm leaving, Tansy. I am leaving you, my job, and Glasgow. In one month I will be in Dubai. I cannot reconcile myself with what you have done." Reuben launched the magazine on to the seat beside her, and left the room.

TWENTY-TWO

It was beginning to become a habit. Craig's visits were now so frequent that he almost considered that Callum's spare room belonged to him. It suited both men, Callum enjoyed Craig's company which was more stimulating than any of his interactions in the staff room, and Craig preferred it to a guest house. Although he felt the odd twinge of conscience that perhaps he was taking too great an advantage of Callum's generosity, he had been reassured by his friend that this was not the case and that he welcomed the disruption to his routine. Throughout the autumn Craig and Taylor were meeting and planning some business enterprises and Craig, used to travelling, happily made the journey knowing that he could stay with Callum.

"It won't be long before you too will be thinking of selling your place in Edinburgh," Callum said one evening as they were clearing dinner.

"You are probably right," Craig admitted. "It's strange how people are drawn back to their roots, but it's not my decision alone."

"You have to go away to appreciate what you once took for granted. I can't imagine ever wanting to move now. A small town is like a family. In a city you can go unnoticed."

Craig measured the coffee grounds into a jug, poured on some boiling water and stirred it twelve times, and then, seeing that Callum was watching, stirred once in the opposite direction. He grinned.

"It is definitely time for me to find somewhere. If you hear of a property let me know. I'll need a place with storage but business is buoyant and prices here are affordable."

Craig followed as Callum picked up the two mugs and took them through to the living room. The furniture was traditional, inherited with the house. The bookcases and armchairs along with the carpets were in good condition, having escaped the misuse inflicted by young children. He noticed that Callum had removed the joyless landscapes that had hung on the walls and replaced them with paintings that he would have chosen with care. He was too much of an artist to consider paintings as wallpaper. Craig saw the juxtaposition as incongruous and wondered why Callum did not stamp his mark on the room as a whole.

"Will you stay here?" Craig asked.

Callum looked surprised.

"The seventies furniture?"

Craig feared that he might have offended his friend. "I won't move and one day I'll get around to modernising. I am beginning to see the place through others' eyes but I only really care about the paintings."

Craig swept his eyes around the walls. He placed his mug on the table and stood up. "What can you tell me about this one?" His attention had been caught by a small frame which, being hidden behind a lamp, was inconspicuous.

"There's something familiar about it." He turned and Callum nodded knowingly.

"Go on," Callum encouraged.

"It's recent, isn't it? It has a contemporary feel."

"Hot off the press."

Craig scrutinised the painting and sat down waiting for Callum to elaborate. "Kerry is selling them. The artist is Jacob's daughter."

Craig leapt to his feet and went back to the painting. "Of course. I should have guessed, and like her father she does not sign them. She grabs your attention, doesn't she? Her touch is lighter but she manages that broad embrace that is her father's hallmark."

"You like it then?"

"She's a winner. What happened to her?"

"Soon after the débâcle, if I can call it that, Abigail and her boyfriend David took off. They've been travelling, from what I heard from John. He took it well although he fretted, wanting David on the boats. She had been in a bit of a mess, I gather, even beforehand. However, Kerry started to hang Abigail's paintings in her shop, they sold, and the girl seemed to settle. She never did return to college."

Callum switched on the television but kept the sound muted. "Where are you going next week? I'm always eager to hear about any emerging artist that you've uncovered."

"To see Eoin. I want to see how his business is reacting to this new scenario or whether we have miscalculated. What happens there could predict developments here."

"Is your business thriving?"

His friend did not want to pry but it was inevitable that he should be curious. "Very much so! You have probably noticed the spring in my step."

"But you haven't changed your car or that old coat of yours."

Craig raised his arm and examined the worn elbow of his jacket. "Can't give the game away, can I? Not yet!" Craig tried to imagine himself driving a sedate family car dressed in a designer jacket, and failed. "I'm unlikely to change, if that reassures you, Callum. Trading is fickle and anyone relying on such a livelihood has to depend on the vagaries of the purchasing public. And they are not dependable.

However, I have to admit that I am relishing this upsurge in activity and having to rely on my intuition."

***

As Craig boarded the train and estimated the hours that it would take to reach the ferry and then cross to Douglas on the Isle of Man, he wished that he could have justified taking a flight. However, once resigned to the journey, he surprised himself by enjoying the experience, and even planned to break his return trip to do a spot of business.

Eoin was waiting on the quay, but Craig became crushed among the queue of passengers as they filed down the gangplank and lost sight of him. As the crowd began to disperse, Craig found Eoin in animated conversation with another passenger and hesitated to intrude. Suddenly Eoin lunged past the stragglers to grasp his hand.

"Really good to see you. I never thought I'd have the pleasure of your company twice in one year." He called across to the friend that he had abandoned. "A rare bird has arrived! A special guest! Forgive me, I must be gone." Craig was warmed by his effusive reception. Perhaps his arrival was an event of note on a small island. "We have quite an evening ahead," Eoin enthused as he strode away from the jetty with Craig. "If it's all the same to you I've tidied my spare room and you can stay with me. The pub is passable and I know you suggested it, but it would please me if you would stay."

"If you are prepared to have me. I have seen enough impersonal hotel rooms. I'll treat you to a meal tonight."

"No need. I've prepared a feast!" declared Eoin.

Eoin had left his shop unattended and now pushed open the door and switched the sign. "No one will come, but it is good to look willing."

Whatever the weather the interior of the shop was gloomy, the October light penetrated where it could through the crowded display window facing the street, but in the late afternoon the room was almost in darkness. "Come through. I can't remember if you've been into my den." Craig had not, on previous occasions, ventured beyond the shop; however, Eoin's house was exactly as he imagined it.

Time had stopped for some forty years; dark wood, steep stairs, low ceilings and ancient furnishings; but it was clean and cared for.

"You live alone?" Craig asked.

"Have done for years. A woman comes and keeps on top of the place for me. She's a gem. It's rare that I have visitors but your arrival has spurred me on to clear up the place. It was needing it, I can tell you!"

Craig followed as Eoin climbed the narrow stairs and then showed him a small room with a single bed. Eoin drew the curtains with their pattern of trains and engines and patted the bed with its child-friendly cover. Craig placed his overnight bag on the single chair and removed his jacket.

"Come down when you're ready. We're going over to Manquill Castle after we've eaten."

When Craig joined him in the kitchen, the table was laid with two wine glasses and with napkins beside the placemats. Eoin had an apron tied untidily around his waist, the strings too long and the pockets askew.

"Manquill Castle?" Craig asked.

"It's quite a landmark on the island. I'm surprised that you have not heard of it."

"I have certainly heard of it," Craig said hurriedly, "but why?"

"I'll let Phillip, the owner, explain. Do sit down."

Craig watched as Eoin lifted a saucepan from the range. He drained the vegetables and placed them into a dish. He then opened the door of one of the lower ovens, releasing a surge of heat and a comforting smell of cottage pie. Finally from another compartment he took out two plates. Craig was transported by these familiar actions to his grandmother's kitchen and suspected that Eoin's range might well be from the same vintage.

"Warm plates. A luxury," Craig commented appreciatively.

Eoin beamed. "These old cookers last for ever. Not much of that modern stuff does, but you and I are attuned to the durable, in our line of work. Tuck in.

"Even for us the market is evolving and how many of today's artists will prove as durable?"

Craig took a few mouthfuls. "Excellent pie." He paused, fork in the air. "You sold all your paintings. Are you planning to speculate in this new market? After all, it was here that it all began."

"You mean buy paintings again? Who can resist? But not in the way that we used to. I am working with the island's national gallery as they purchase paintings to replace the original stock."

"A nice budget I should imagine?"

"It's been the most satisfying work of my career and the new collection is drawing in people as never before."

"Have you thought how this could be maintained, once the initial novelty has worn off?"

"Wait until we meet Phillip and all will become clear."

It was dark as Eoin and Craig left Douglas for Manquill Castle. The unlit road, once they had left the town, was narrow with headlights alone warning of oncoming traffic. After several miles Eoin applied the brakes until they were almost at a standstill. "There's a turning to the left around here." His headlights caught two large gates which were open but almost obscured by untrimmed rhododendron bushes.

"It's a long time since those gates were closed," Craig commented. This easy access reduced Craig's apprehension at meeting the owner. He had met many illustrious and wealthy people in the course of his career but with the seismic shift in the dealing world he was not as self-assured as he might have been a year earlier. The drive was rutted with potholes from where the water dripped from overhanging trees, and the grass verges were ragged. After several minutes of careful driving Eoin turned up a slight hill at a fork in the drive and the castle loomed above them. The tyres crunched on the gravel and Eoin drew up under an arched porch. Two lamps illuminated a large wooden door.

A dog barked as the door opened swiftly from inside and a young man in a knitted sweater and worn cords, with a spaniel running ahead around the car, walked towards them smiling as if no one else could make him as delighted.

Eoin was still emerging from the car when Phillip reached over the open door to shake his hand. Craig, whose preconceived image of an ancient codger was rapidly being replaced by the reality of an energetic young man, was not given time to speak. "You're Craig. I've heard so much about you. From Eoin. Come in."

Craig deduced that Eoin must have a working relationship with Phillip. He wondered in what capacity he was involved and assumed that he was about to find out. It amused him that all of them, he, Eoin and Taylor, were having to adapt and embrace the new art scene at a time when they thought that they would be transitioning into steady retirement. Craig felt grateful for the chance to meet and interact with young blood and, from what he had already witnessed, Phillip was a congenial and approachable man who had already reanimated Eoin.

Once through the door, they entered the hall which was panelled exclusively in wood with doors inset so that only their brass handles denoted their existence. From gold embossed frames ancestral portraits peered out impassively, interspersed with stags' heads mounted and inscribed. Walking over the chequered black and white tiles, Craig smothered a shiver as he reacted to the chill.

Noticing Craig's indrawing of breath Phillip reassured him, "You get used to it. It's warmer in here." He opened one of the doors and the heat from a generous log fire greeted them. Phillip and Eoin immediately began to discuss business, allowing Craig to wander around the room.

The drawing room had the imprint of many genera-tions. The chintz curtains and the upholstery reflected the taste of Phillip's predecessors, but the room was well lit and the artefacts tastefully arranged. On a tray inside the door were several glasses and a decanter and after a while Phillip absent-mindedly filled three glasses with whisky. He handed one to Craig who was studying a painting beside the fireplace. "I'm neglecting you. How anti-social of me. I keep that for sentimental reasons. It is one of my mother's."

"She had talent. Have both your parents died?" Craig was curious that Phillip should have already inherited the castle.

"She's alive, but my grandfather did not believe in handing over to a daughter, so this all came to me."

"Did you want it?"

"No choice." Phillip looked at Craig as if this fact were self-evident. "That's how it is, and now it is up to me to make a go of it. That's why I was so lucky to meet Eoin."

Eoin heard his name and Phillip beckoned him over.

They each selected an armchair. Eoin lowered himself carefully, balancing his glass. "My knees, you know!" He grimaced. "I'll leave it to you to explain, Phillip."

Phillip sat forward in his chair. "It's all thanks to Eoin. When I heard that the Tynwald really had passed the hundred-year law, you see up to then people dismissed it as a rumour, I called on Eoin. I reckoned he might be able to advise me. To my mind the law seemed to have as many advantages as disadvantages."

Eoin chipped in. "Phillip had to come and see me at some point, anyway, to have his pictures registered for his International Art Number. It is similar to the ISBN which is allocated to every book that is published. I'd secured that contract." Craig thought that Eoin looked, with reason, pleased with himself.

"While we were discussing the pros and cons Eoin suggested that we might go into partnership."

Eoin explained, "Instead of a permanent exhibition as we have had on the island for decades, I proposed the idea of moving whole exhibitions. Move the paintings to the people instead of expecting people to travel to the paintings. Phillip persuaded the committee that if other galleries followed suit we should gain a reputation for being at the forefront with solutions in response to the new scenario. Just imagine! Six exhibitions a year from all over the world, here, in Douglas!" Eoin's eyes gleamed and Phillip looked questioningly for Craig's response.

"You should have this ready and be the first to promote it."

"Eoin had money to invest and I had ideas that I wanted to develop."

This seemed simple economic sense to Craig. He concluded that Eoin was a wily old bird with more stashed away than one might have guessed. "Your ideas. Can I hear them?"

"Let me show you!" Phillip's movements were fluid as he stood up and moved to the door. "We've already put one into action. I've converted the ballroom. It has proved an excellent location." Craig braced himself for the blast of cold air.

Eoin followed in his own time as Phillip led Craig through a maze of corridors. "This is the new venture," Phillip announced. "Here is the café." The room was still warm from the day's occupants. "We have had a lot of customers today, but that will change by the end of the month and it will be quiet until Christmas."

The floor space was filled with tables and chairs with an extensive counter for operating the machines and assembling food. The furniture was a hotchpotch which complimented the atmosphere of an old building. At one end of the ballroom Phillip had hung a medley of paintings.

"Eoin found the furniture and I gathered up the paintings from around the castle. The collection in the library and drawing room we have left in place. Eoin believes that they would look lost if they were out of context, and since those rooms were only used for entertaining Eoin suggested that I open them to the public." Phillip led them up a staircase and into the library.

"Will you charge people to see the paintings?" Craig, ever practical, wondered how Phillip could capitalise on his collection.

"Not downstairs. That's a taster. They'll pay to go upstairs. People want to see the inside of houses even more than they want to look at paintings. Even so, I expect to make my money in the café."

They stood and admired the library where leather bound

books filled shelves from floor to ceiling, and where the once priceless paintings decorated the walls. Craig noticed that there were no discreet rails of rope cordoning off the treasures. "No rails," Phillip told him. "If someone wants to destroy or remove a painting no flimsy barrier will deter them. I have a feeling that if you respect people, and make an assumption that they come here to enjoy these wonderful works, they will respond in a civilised fashion."

Eoin said, "On the whole, only those who are interested will be prepared to pay and visit these rooms. This is only one part of our business partnership." He looked to Phillip for his approval.

Once they were in the drawing room Phillip added more logs to the fire and then filled their glasses. "It's lonely here," Phillip told Craig. "The island is small and looking after the estate does not bring me into contact with many people, except when I am on the farm. The café runs on its own momentum and I must say it is grand having staff coming and going. You've no idea of the gossip that I am privy to! Art is in vogue at the moment, it's in the news, people are re-thinking their relationship to it and are becoming less intimidated. Eoin and I launched a tentative foray into the holiday market. We delivered some flyers to the hotels and holiday houses offering a day's tuition. This has been popular, especially on wet days."

Craig could see the potential. "You'll soon be having artists in residence."

"That's our hope."

"Why do you think that this was not done before?"

"The climate wasn't right. Neither for my grandparents' generation, nor the public. Drawing was for children, or retirement. You were expected to be proficient. Since the explosion of cookery courses, which people are prepared to sign up to with no prior knowledge, they are seeking other interests."

Craig and Eoin finished their drinks and stood up. "We've taken enough of your time."

Craig gave Phillip's shoulder a friendly punch. "I'd like to hear about any new projects and I'm keen to help. I have a wide network of contacts. Who can turn down free advertising?"

Phillip walked with them towards the hall. "I've been following the articles by Tansy Witt but their content has changed. I wonder whether her remit has been altered as she seems to have been reined in. Her articles have lost their sparkle and originality. Have you noticed?"

Eoin walked ahead, but Craig stopped, thoughtful. "No, I have not read her magazine recently, not since the upset in the summer."

"Upset?" Phillip queried, but Eoin was already saying goodbye and Craig followed his cue.

"Tansy Witt? What's happened?" Eoin asked once they were driving along the road.

"It's a long story," Craig began.

The next day, as Craig headed north he puzzled over Phillip's comment regarding Tansy. However, he was more excited by the momentum that the new law had gathered. Eoin had related that rumours within the art world had purportedly witnessed salerooms and antique shops abroad showing a huge increase in commodities passing through their hands. He was keen to share this information with his circle of friends and he would suggest to Taylor that they meet.

***

"Taylor. You look younger every time I see you. Your

venture must be thriving." Taylor's business was a success
but an acknowledgement was always welcome.

"It comes with its fair share of headaches. I was not
expecting it to be plain sailing. These are my new acquisi-
tions, I am in the process of arranging my next show. They
are all by artists who have hardly a sale between them.
You can't imagine how stimulating it has been. I'll start
with the big wall and then we'll go upstairs. I've even some
paintings from the students. See what you think and then
deliver your verdict."

As they walked up the stairs Taylor asked, "What was the
news from the Isle?"

"It's snowballing. That's the word on the ground and
from what I heard from Eoin. Other governments are
debating and exploring the Tynwald law and its repercussions."

Taylor nodded slowly. "We dealers need to be ahead. If it
is adopted by the smaller parliaments it is only a matter of
time before others will follow. It stands to reason. Everyone
gains. Well, almost everyone!"

The atmosphere of the upper gallery felt clinical due to
Taylor's choice of pale wood and cream paintwork. He had
furnished it with armchairs and sofas in primary colours
and arranged piles of art magazines on the coffee tables.
He allowed Craig time to study the paintings, although he
hovered, eager to hear his opinion.

"Give me a moment to do another spot of talent eval-
uation." Craig moved methodically from one exhibit to
another. "Many of them are easy on the eye. That must
draw people here."

"I've a faithful core that support each exhibition and
I've encouraged them to make suggestions so that they are
involved. It has reaped its reward. I have eyes everywhere

and they have formed a society which now organise all the opening nights. Has any artist caught your attention?"

"This one!" Craig turned towards Taylor. "It's most unusual. It's only two feet by three yet the landscape covers several miles of coastline. The artist has the ability to paint the lighthouse over there on the headland as clearly as the litter and pebbles on the beach."

Taylor was sitting on a lemon-yellow sofa and Craig joined him. "If you scout the artists and I undertook the finances and promotion, we could actually commission work."

"Old-fashioned patronage?"

Craig answered eagerly, "Why not?" Then he challenged Taylor. "Have you any alternative proposals?"

"I was on the same tack. Promoting and encouraging whichever artists strike me as having potential. I think that we can come to an agreement." Taylor sat back and surveyed his collection, he felt proprietorial and in some way beholden to his artists. Meanwhile Craig's eyes were caught by the cover of a magazine. He picked it up. It featured one of Jacob's paintings. On the table was every back copy of *Inside and Out* magazine spanning nearly two years.

"Is she still writing? Tansy Witt?" Craig asked.

"I believe so. I'm planning to invite her down again. I thought that she might like to do a follow-up article. After all, she was the catalyst, wasn't she?"

Taylor was disturbed to see that Craig was hesitant and appeared to avoid the question by asking another.

"Can you spare these for a few weeks, until I call again?" He indicated the pile of magazines.

"Of course! Are you going to tell me why?"

"I will, when I've discovered what I need to know." Craig

was unusually obtuse.

Taylor reverted to their previous conversation. "I'll come back to you with an outline of how we could work together when you return the magazines."

TWENTY-THREE

The sun streamed into the flat through dirt-encrusted windows. Were it not for their generous height the amount of light that they admitted would have required the flat to be permanently lit by electric bulbs. Tansy, laden with a shoulder bag, two plastic supermarket carriers and with her key in one hand, struggled through the door and into the kitchen. She sighed with irritation because once again she had failed to avoid the woman in the flat below and been waylaid. It seemed that Tansy's private life was of supreme interest but, either because Tansy was skilful at protecting it, or because she had none to protect, so far the woman's enquiries had elicited no satisfactory results.

Switching on the kettle, Tansy took out a mug and poured some instant coffee. She removed her scarf, woolly hat and jacket and shivered as she hung them on a hook in the hall. In the living room she bent down by the gas fire and reached for the button. She heard the comforting minor explosion as the flame caught, and remained crouched to watch the blue light turn to yellow. Again she sighed. This was not how she had envisaged her career as a journalist. It was not how she had planned her working days in Glasgow. Although she often travelled around the country, in essence the routine was the same. At the end of the day she was alone.

After her finals she and her friends had pledged to keep in touch, but many had moved away, and she and Reuben had been sufficient company for one another. She had not made overtures to create new friends and now she felt the lack.

The kettle boiled and Tansy returned to the kitchen. She opened the fridge, only to remember that the milk was still unpacked. Mechanically she opened and shut cupboards, neatly stacking her purchases, and then folded the bags into a container under the sink. Taking up her coffee, she wandered back to the living room and thought how much she had looked forward to having Florrie to share her flat. Somehow she had not made the effort to find someone else. It would have been a pleasure to mentor the younger girl, and show her around the city. She might even have helped her decide on her future career. Florrie was unlikely to have become a disruptive party-going flatmate. Tansy could not imagine any of Jacob's family shedding their steady upbringing and changing character to such an extreme, but she feared that Florrie would be working and living in a hotel with an unenviable routine, feeling equally lonely. Unlike the Florrie of her imagination, Tansy at least had a job that challenged her and from her shoulder bag she pulled out her schedule for the next day. She ran her eyes down the typing to see what preparations were needed. She held the paper long after she had absorbed the information. Some of the allure in chasing stories had gone. She remembered the sense of exhilaration that each assignment had given her, how on arriving home she would be scribbling her first draft even while making her evening meal. She recalled the excitement of meeting a new artist and then describing her impressions and communicating her reactions to her readers.

However, since the events of the summer Tansy had shied away from work that included interviewing artists and had volunteered to cover exhibitions in town centres and libraries. This was the staple route for amateur artists and inevitably these shows contained pictures of mixed ability about which Tansy often laboured to find anything original to say. She suspected that she was becoming formulaic and that her writing no longer evidenced the spark for which she had become noted.

Back in the kitchen Tansy put some spaghetti in a pan and opened a jar of Bolognese sauce, despising herself for her lack of effort. Yet everything seemed to require effort. She wondered if it was time for her to look for a job with another magazine. Her parents were urging her to apply in London, and only in part because it was an easier destination for them. She felt restless but attributed it to Reuben's departure for Dubai. Her stubborn streak prevented her from throwing away the position that she now held in *Inside and Out*.

Tansy was unnecessarily brusque in her movements as she dished the food on to her plate. She could feel her breath deepen and as she tipped the saucepan into the sink and ran the water her hands shook. Taking control of her emotions, she carried her plate of unappetising spaghetti into the living room. She ate mechanically, staring beyond the coffee table and even beyond the display of photographs that covered the opposite wall. Once again she revisited her last conversation with Reuben. Had she really been as underhand and devious as he had made out? She had not intended to capitalise on her acquaintance with Jacob although she had to admit that she had been starstruck. This might have clouded her judgement but no amount of analysis of the lead-up to their row explained Reuben's over-reaction. She wished that she knew how Jacob viewed it. If he too felt betrayed by her, then she had made a gross misjudgement and that would direct her to change to writing for another paper, but she had no contacts to help her ascertain his mood. Instead she comforted herself that her editorial office had never questioned the content of her articles, or their source.

Briefly she allowed herself to ask what Reuben's attitude to their argument might be now. Would he regret saying that she had destroyed whatever had bound them together? What blindness on Reuben's part prevented him from considering the episode from her viewpoint? Without Reuben in her life Tansy knew that her writing had become bland, but she wondered if it was only because of Reuben's exit, maybe it was because of her loss of contact with Jacob.

She gazed at the wall and her eyes focused on a photograph of Reuben at the mill. She could not bring herself to remove any memories of him. In the photograph he looked proud and happy. Behind him hung a painting that she had not registered before because she always searched his face to scrutinise his thoughts. The painting was one where the cornfields, raised on the surface, met the sky and the sea. As she examined the painting she remembered the day that Jacob had shown it to her, and she could hear him speaking.

Suddenly she sprang up to find her pad and scrabbled in her bag for a pen. She still had something to say and she would not be held mute, not by Jacob and certainly not by Reuben. She was confident that *Inside and Out* would print any article that she wrote, such had been the success of the issue featuring Jacob's Art. She would not display that particular painting this time, but she would echo his words and justify her motivation in revealing the work of the reclusive artist. With one final look at the painting she sat back in her chair, placed her pad on her lap, and started writing.

***

For someone who had barely left her home town, rarely boarded a train, and never been on an aeroplane, Dubai Airport came as a shock. Abigail, having already negotiated Glasgow and Heathrow, presumed that all airports would be replicas, but on emerging from this leg of her journey realised that she could no longer make assumptions.

She stood, with David beside her, transfixed by the cathedral-sized proportions, the overpowering glare of lights and the fake grandiosity, while around them passengers circled purposefully. That Reuben was able to adapt to this pretend world, Abigail doubted, but neither had she expected him to carry out his threat to leave Glasgow.

To Abigail's surprise it had not taken David more than a few days to agree with her suggestion that they work abroad. "It's only for a few months," he rationalised. "I've talked it over with my Dad. He can spare me. My Mum's keen. I think she wishes that she was travelling to Australia. She said that they never had the opportunity."

It was Kerry whose innocent remark had set the idea in motion. When handing Abigail a packet with her earnings for the week she asked where she was taking off to with her well-earned riches. Abigail repeated this to David and said that if they worked hard, along with their savings, they could afford the airfare.

Somehow, once Reuben had taken the job in Dubai the family felt fragmented. Florrie moved out to live and work in the Metropole Hotel and Matty delved into her school-work as soon as she arrived home off the bus. Abigail found her distant and elusive and so whenever David was unable to drive her into the country to paint her landscapes, Abigail worked alongside her father in his studio. When she was outside she would sketch or watercolour. She worked rapidly but felt slightly ashamed at the ease with which she could produce and sell these paintings. However, with her father and under his purist influence, she developed her technique and sharpened her eye. She wondered occasionally if her father disapproved of her mercenary approach, but he never criticised her. Yet watching his absorption in his own work she questioned whether she should be less calculating. She consciously attempted to counterbalance her pleasing landscapes by exploring a more serious style and she hoped that this was the reason her father was content, because he merely passed the occasional gentle comment on her financial acumen.

When Abigail announced to her parents her intention to travel, they raised no objections. She smiled as she imagined their reactions to the vulgar ostentation of Dubai Airport's ultra-modern arrival hall, but she was, nevertheless, impressed. The homogeneous grandeur and attention to detail drew a gasp, which was reciprocated by David. It was while they stood, stunned by architecture so alien, that Reuben found them. "Wait until you see Dubai itself," he told them. That evening, still seated at the table in a restaurant overlooking the city of Dubai, Abigail challenged Reuben.

"So what happened?" Abigail asked. That it was her brother, usually so frugal and antagonistic to affectation, who had introduced them to haute cuisine was an irony that was not lost on either of them.

"You mean the venue?" Reuben was deliberately obtuse, fending off an inquisition that he knew was due, and smiled wryly.

"That, too," admitted Abigail, "although I expect that was just for show?"

Reuben nodded, but knew that there was more to her question than a desire to know why he was treating them to one of Dubai's most celebrated restaurants. He knew his sister too well to think that she would not ask about his behaviour in the summer. David nursed his wine glass, waiting for Abigail to tackle her brother. Their conversation on the journey had forewarned him.

"What happened to you that you headed for this centre of materialism? Why the sudden departure? We assume it was because of Tansy? But why? And why here?"

"Here, because it is the opposite of there. Our home town and the way that we were brought up. Why?" Reuben looked speculatively across at Abigail whose expression was inscrutable, and at David who avoided his stare. "Why?" he repeated.

Abigail held his eyes, determined to extract an answer. "You have to take some responsibility for the upheaval that the family's been through."

Rather than answer directly, Reuben drew on a narrative which he had already prepared, anticipating Abigail's question. "There is a meaning beyond a piece of art, or music. There is more to art than the finished picture and more to music than its manuscript. An idealist creates art for its own sake. It should move you, and then change you. It should speak to the inner spiritual world that is within each person."

To cover his embarrassment, fearing that he had revealed too much of himself, he turned to David. "Tansy did not understand that artists are inspired from within themselves and are only interested in what they create and not in its value."

David ran his finger around the rim of his glass. "I understand what you are saying, but wasn't Tansy trying to enlarge the audience that might benefit from Jacob's work?"

Calling Jacob by his name somehow made the argument academic and removed much of the emotion with which it was charged. "She should have understood," Reuben countered defensively. "She spent a good many hours listening to Jacob's views and theories."

"As a journalist," Abigail interposed, "how could it be otherwise? She was new to the scene. We had been indoctrinated from birth. To us it was natural that art could be created for its own sake. I felt that I had betrayed Jacob's ideals by selling my landscapes, but Tansy would see selling as a logical reason for painting."

"Jacob was a purist, Tansy should have recognised that and not attempted to launch his work by creating a mystery."

"It is a mystery. That's its appeal," Abigail insisted.

Reuben showed his exasperation. "An appeal that ultimately sells magazines. That's hardly art for art's sake." He was voicing the reasons for his actions that he had been rehearsing since his final argument with Tansy. "Someone needed to protect the family from exposure to the media."

"Have you considered Tansy's motives?" Abigail asked. "Although it is contrary to our understanding of his perspective, is it not possible that Tansy wrote about Jacob with an altruistic purpose?"

Reuben detected an overlying anxiety which gave extra weight to her question and he became aware that on his response depended the healing of the rift in their family.

It was a curious setting for a mediation. Amongst the glitter and modernity of their surroundings Abigail attempted to effect a resolution to a split that balanced ethics and moral convictions. It was hardly an environment conducive to resolving an argument where ideology and practicality clashed.

"Despite your view of life and your innate prejudices

you have to decide whether you can forgive Tansy," David said bluntly, when the silence had dragged on.

Reuben recognised that they were forcing the issue. He had run away so that he could avoid confrontation with Tansy or with the problem that she had posed, but if the events of the summer were to draw to a conclusion, he no longer had that option.

"I think that Tansy and I need to talk," he said.

TWENTY-FOUR

Craig was in constant communication with Jacob. Sales of Jacob's paintings had gone well but media interest in him and his whereabouts had dwindled to a trickle. Tourists had disappeared and the journalists had, weeks before, exhausted every angle of his story.

In the upstairs studio, Craig was taking his time perusing the recent collection of paintings that Jacob had assembled for him to sell. Craig was beginning to see them through Jacob's eyes and was learning how to interpret them. At the beginning he had seen the paintings as a stake in the chase for a new market, but now he wondered how he could have been blind to their power. He enjoyed them for their own sake and not because the commercial climate was changing. He had found an artist with real talent and his appreciation of Jacob's work, probably due to years of being in tune with his clients, had been vindicated. He remembered what had spurred him on in his early days of trading: the excitement of uncovering hidden treasures, and with Jacob he knew that he had discovered gold. He did not care, particularly, about their potential financial value, but he did relish the status that he was gaining from launching his work on to an unsuspecting world.

He found it hard to express this emotion to Jacob. "I am overwhelmed," he said. "I am not the effusive type, and I don't express myself well, but these paintings of yours are seriously spectacular." He looked sideways at Jacob whose features, usually so impenetrable, betrayed the hint of a smile. "They grow on a person. I am becoming addicted!" At that, Jacob, beneath his thick beard, grinned contentedly.

Craig picked up one of Jacob's smaller paintings and tipped it towards the light, fascinated by the changes produced on the canvas.

"Perhaps it was all for the best," Jacob admitted.

Craig's head jerked round and he looked questioningly to see if he had understood correctly what Jacob implied. "You think so?" Craig appeared to come to a decision. He put down the canvas and went over to the door where he had left his briefcase. He carried it across to Jacob's large work table which was covered with scrunched rags, pots of brushes, thinners and tubes of paint. "Can I?" He indicated a small area that was free from clutter, put down his briefcase and opened it. Then he pulled up a chair.

Jacob dragged another from where it was supporting a canvas. "What have you got to show me?" He started cleaning a brush absent-mindedly.

"I have been puzzled by Tansy Witt."

Jacob stopped his actions with the rag momentarily, and then continued, from which Craig assumed that he too could proceed.

"We have a young girl with little or no knowledge of her subject, yet she has a regular feature in a glossy magazine, and finally a piece in a major newspaper. Someone must have been feeding her ideas. I went back over all her articles. I have them here, from April a year ago until now."

Jacob placed the rag and brush amongst the others on the table and seemed to withdraw into himself. Craig deliberated how to approach Jacob with a suspicion that had grown into more than a possibility.

"Tansy is still writing for *Inside and Out*, although her

articles since the débâcle are quite tame." He paused, hoping that, although he was referring to the unfortunate events of the summer, Jacob would allow him to continue. Jacob acknowledged with the slightest movement of his head, and Craig hurried on, "Until this month, but I'll come to that."

From out of his briefcase, held together with a large paper clip, Craig brought a stack of shiny papers, each one torn along one edge, and then took out the top article and read aloud the title. "'Should there be a prohibition of sales of paintings over one hundred years old?' This was the article which sparked the original interest in the Isle of Man. Eoin, a colleague in the trade, showed it to some friends, one or two of whom are members of the Manx parliament. You could say that this, her first piece, started the momentum."

Craig handed the article to Jacob, who read the piece through to the end and shook his head. "What next?"

"'Children should be given formal instruction in drawing and painting at a young age.'" He passed the paper to Jacob. "Then there's 'Art need only to be enjoyed visually.'" Craig began passing page after page. "Here's another. 'Why artists are handicapped from earning a living.' Or, 'Comparing musicians who are entitled to teach once they have qualified to artists who have no similar diploma.'"

"Then we come to your exhibition and the first inkling of moves afoot to bring in a new law in Tynwald, which she writes about in July. I am partly guilty there because I sent her to speak to Eoin. Then there is Taylor's planned theatre to make people really look at paintings. Where did that idea originate?"

He pointed out others. "'To be an artist you have to have something to say.' 'Drawing is vital for the young.' And 'Is Art a luxury?'"

Jacob sifted through the articles, stopping at one, returning to another, until finally he reached the last one on the pile. "There should be some more. The ones that she has written since she wrote the 'Mysterious red dots' story." This was the article that had sparked the media interest. Craig knew that it was not easy for Jacob, with all the associated memories, to ask about it.

"As I said, they are innocuous, one covers the Edinburgh Festival and another some craft fair and none of them are in her usual style, which is curious but it's this month's contribution which triggered my visit to you. See what you think."

Craig gave him time to read it. The article was entitled, 'What price Art?' He crossed the room to take a further look at the painting that Jacob was working on. It was so large that no easel could support it and Jacob had cleared one wall to make a space for the canvas. The subject was a landscape with blocks of brown and yellow in the foreground and smaller blocks of blue in the distance suggesting a harbour. Despite the deep colours none of Jacob's pictures were morbid, all in some way celebrated nature or life, and they gave Craig a feeling of optimism. He wondered if he had overstepped the boundaries by approaching Jacob with Tansy's writings, particularly the final one, and whether it was presumptuous of him to attempt to act as mediator.

In her article Tansy had set out a riposte to the accusation that she had invaded an artist's privacy. She claimed that she had given him an outlet for his work, work whose essence was communication. Artists, she wrote, like musicians, had an inner force which drove their creative instincts, but whose ultimate aim was to communicate with others. Whether it was sculpture, or paint, or lyrics, or theatre, humans seek to interact with people around them and need a conduit to express this primeval emotion. If an artist, for whatever reason, was unable to share their work then they were only partially fulfilled. Tansy, without mentioning her own part in the affair of Jacob's Art, argued that, at some level, there was justification for the role of a journalist.

Jacob placed the article on the table and flattened it with his hands. "An artist has to communicate, because if they are a genuine artist, they have something to say," he quoted, but made no comment. "I think that Deborah should read these." He moved towards the stairs. "I'll show you round my vegetable patch while she does so."

Craig waited until he returned from the house. Jacob reached for his leather jerkin and Craig watched, amused, as he fastened his buttons through inadequate and torn buttonholes. Jacob thrust his hands into his pockets and led the way down the steps. At the foot of the steps he stopped, retrieved some grassy fronds with delicate white flowers from one of the pockets, and turned with his hand outstretched.

"Here, smell this. It is not something you will find in your city. It's gone to seed." Craig took the sprigs of parsley and sensed that with this gesture Jacob was re-establishing their relationship on their old footing, and felt hopeful.

They set off in silence. After a while Jacob spoke. "The garden and orchard have gone to sleep, but a few vegetables still remain through the winter. I have broccoli, brussels sprouts and parsnips." Jacob pointed out straggling plants and the barely visible fronds of parsnips. Elsewhere the earth had been dug over. The heavy soil, healthy and weed-free, seemed already to be inviting next year's produce. "The apple trees are too old to prune but they and the plums and pears give a good crop." Jacob led Craig to the shed where he stored potatoes in sacks and carrots in sand and, taking an apple from one of the pallets, handed it to Craig. "These will see us until around the end of February." They crunched their apples companionably while Craig subdued an urge to ask Jacob what he had deduced from Tansy's writings.

Craig also pondered how Deborah would react and whether she was open to the possibility of forgiving Tansy. He wanted to assuage his own guilt in the events that had led up to the media assault on Jacob and Deborah's home, and he determined to admit that he was partly to blame because of his involvement with Tansy's quest. However, he knew that he had to give both Jacob and Deborah time to absorb her writing and this tour of Jacob's plot was timely.

"We keep twelve chickens and they lay well. We have enough eggs even when the family are here. Remind me to give you a dozen before you go."

When they entered the kitchen Deborah was sitting in Jacob's chair with the pile of papers scattered on the table in front of her. "I wondered where you two were." She looked up and smiled.

Jacob indicated to Craig to sit with them. "Well?" he asked Deborah.

Craig fidgeted and then could not hold back. "Do you think someone has been supplying this girl with ideas? A young person who knows so little could not write like this."

"You are right!" Deborah's cheerful demeanour did not change. "We know where she got these ideas, don't we Jacob!" Craig saw a look of unanimity pass between them. "This is pure Jacob!" she explained. "Tansy has absorbed his ideas and written them up in her own style."

Craig gave a deep sigh of relief. "My hunch that she had absorbed someone else's ideas was correct, but I never would have guessed that they were yours." He looked in wonder at Jacob.

"You've not yet been around long enough, Craig, to be indoctrinated," Deborah teased him.

Craig said, still unconvinced, "If Tansy has got her ideas from you does that not make you angry with her?"

Deborah answered, "Not any more." She looked at Jacob for confirmation. "Once the season was over the tourists stopped trailing up our lane. Everything passes eventually. In our case it took a few months, but no one's been harmed."

This was the opening Craig was waiting for. "It seems to me that there have, in fact, been many benefits." Deborah looked interested and Jacob remained inscrutable. "There's Andrew and his projects which have enhanced the college. Taylor's change of emphasis from insurance to his gallery has provided him with a challenge and filled the gap in his life." Jacob nodded thoughtfully. Deborah was thinking how Abigail had benefitted from the sale of her paintings through Gerald noticing them by David's desk and telling Kerry. Jacob meanwhile was thinking how Reuben's foray into the commercial world had knocked some sense into him so that he was exploring other avenues of employment. "And I have heard a rumour that Andrew is thinking of retiring so that he can paint, and Gerald is front runner for the post," Craig added.

"What about the girls? Matty and Florrie?" Craig then asked. "Were they adversely affected?"

"Matty?" Deborah exclaimed. "She's just typical of her age and she found it anything but upsetting. She was mainly irked that her father refused any photographs."

"And Florrie?"

Again it was Deborah who replied, "She's annoyed that Reuben split with Tansy and spoiled everything she had planned. Tansy had offered her a room in her flat and Florrie could have moved to Glasgow. As it is she has to live and work in a hotel."

"What about this law?" Jacob asked finally. "The one that they have on the Isle of Man? You speak as if it might happen here?"

"That was the information David gleaned from Lauren," Craig confirmed.

Jacob chuckled. Deborah sat back in her chair and her eyes twinkled as she said to Craig, "Who would believe it? Someone taking Jacob's ramblings seriously."

Craig corrected her, "Perhaps not ramblings after all." He was still concerned for Tansy, however. She seemed to be the only one who had been harmed by the events, even if much of it had been of her making. "I have an apology to make." He paused. "I put Tansy on the path to that article in the Sunday paper. I warned her that the repercussions might not be what she wanted or expected, but no true journalist can resist a story."

Jacob was slow to reply. "I have been thinking about the final article. If I am to be fair, she has a point. Perhaps we have a duty to expose our art to a critical public." Jacob looked towards Deborah to gauge her reaction. "We can't live in a cocoon if someone gives us a chance to launch our work on the world. It is, I believe, what fundamentally we are here to do. To communicate through our art, and if the reaction is adverse, then it is something that we have to accept."

Deborah's mood had sobered while Jacob spoke. The light-hearted atmosphere had dissipated now that they were, in effect, judging Tansy. "I can forgive her," she said. "She made a mistake but she is young. She's only harmed herself."

Craig waited for Jacob's verdict. "I can't blame the girl. I think, although she was misguided, she did it all with the best of motives. I'd be a poor man if I allowed myself to bear a grudge. As it is I can only feel sorry for her."

With this assessment by Jacob on the events of the summer, Craig was certain that he, too, had been forgiven.

TWENTY-FIVE

As Tansy entered Taylor's gallery, she regretted her decision to cover his new exhibition. Although there was no reason for Taylor to know the repercussions of her newspaper article in the summer, or even that it had been published, those events suddenly overwhelmed her and she stood uncertain, almost ready to retreat.

Taylor was, however, welcoming and his kindly manner reduced her fears. "Have you had a busy autumn? All the venues start up in earnest, don't they? It was good of you to make time for me."

Taylor, immaculately dressed in a suit and tie, shook her hand warmly and while he removed her coat he said, "Coffee or paintings first?"

It was a long time since Tansy had felt such paternal solicitude. "Pictures! Then we can discuss them over coffee."

"Splendid!"

On the upper gallery Tansy was still concentrating on her notes, jotting down her impressions from the exhibition and the background to the artists supplied by Taylor when he called, "Coffee?"

She folded her notes and stuffed them into her hold-all and made her way across to the lemon-yellow sofa and scarlet-red armchairs. On the long blue leather-covered table, beside a tray, were piles of *Inside and Out*. Tansy felt herself tremble and then blush. "Do you keep every copy?"

"Probably," Taylor answered her cheerfully, handing her a mug.

Holding it between her hands she studied the design, a series of Lowry figures, distractedly.

"Help yourself to milk."

She continued to stare at the mug.

"You should be proud of what you have written," he said gently. "Craig told me that it caused a bit of a rift."

"Craig? Oh yes!" Tansy nodded and picked up the milk jug. With her head turned away she poured the milk. "I miscalculated, you know."

"We all do at times, but some good usually results."

His soothing tone helped and Tansy faced him. "Do you really think so? Craig did tell me that Jacob and Deborah understand."

"I'm sure they do. Why don't you go and see them?" He leant back in his chair as if to give her time.

"I'll think about it," Tansy responded eventually, smiling gratefully, but she had already made up her mind.

***

The path was lined by gorse which had lost its blazing yellow flowers. It was overgrown with brambles whose long shoots still held a few withered berries, and whose leaves were tinged with a heartening red. The grass along its edges was no longer checked by trampling feet and grew unkempt with the odd flower still blooming. Underfoot the soft earth was wet until Tansy emerged on to the rocks which formed a peninsular with the bay on one side and small coves on the other. Layers of rock had been tipped vertically millennia ago and walking along them was hazardous. The sea pinks and the bird's-foot trefoil from the summer were gone. Reuben had stood there with her, naming the birds, the islands, the distant hills of Cumbria and the whereabouts of Ireland and the Isle of Man.

Tansy perched on the exposed point which jutted out into the sea, her hair blowing away from her face which she lifted up to feel the breeze. The tide had been low, that day with Reuben, and they had walked over the sand to the stony beach and across the grassy mound of the island to the other side. They had sat for a while on the warm rocks with the gulls above, the waves slapping and slurping in and out of the pools, content in each other's company.

It was almost high tide and unless you had seen it, you could not know that there was a causeway to the island. A boat was sailing towards it, perhaps to go fishing; it was too late in the year for pleasure boats. These were the places of Reuben's childhood and she hoped by revisiting them she might understand him better and attempt to discover how this landscape had contributed to the part of Reuben that she could never reach. She also needed to prepare herself to meet Jacob again.

Abruptly she turned and retraced her steps. She would explore the glen. It might not give her any answers, but it would delay her arrival at her ultimate destination.

From the vantage of the great boulder that overlooked the glen, the loch, narrow and bounded on both sides by steep hills, was peat brown and seemingly bottomless. The murky sky, pierced with spotlights of sun, lit the scene like a stage. As she watched, the shafts of light picked out sheep grazing, or a burn snaking down a gully, or ripples trembling on the surface of the water.

The path followed the burn which was one of many that filled the loch, but it was the one that Reuben had chosen. The bracken was now a dirty orange and the fronds were bent so that more of the landscape was revealed. The sound of the burn was more distinct because the rainfall had increased its volume. The rowan had turned pink, with red berries hanging like decorations. How could Reuben, brought up in this idyll, feel such anger where here there was such harmony. Could he maintain that anger towards her, she puzzled. And what about Jacob, would he understand? Craig's recent communication hinted at a less censorious interpretation of those events and she sensed that he was in favour of her meeting Jacob again. What had become clear to her was that, until she established his view of her actions, she could not begin to find a new direction for her life.

She walked steadily until she had composed herself sufficiently to knock on the door of Reuben's home. The moment that the door opened, Tansy's prepared first sentence evaporated. Florrie, her expression hovering between disbelief and caution, said shyly, "Hello, Tansy. Won't you come in?"

Tansy stood in the familiar surroundings of Reuben's home but this time it was empty. It seemed that the family was in the sitting room. It occurred to her that Reuben might be with them when Deborah, closing the door behind her, approached.

"It has been a long time, dear," she said. "Take off your coat and we'll have a quiet talk, and you can tell us why you are here. Shall I fetch Jacob?"

Tansy nodded. Words seemed to elude her. Her anxiety heightened as she waited.

"You'll be here about the summer," Jacob said in his deep sonorous voice, "with Reuben away we've had no news of you. So I'm curious. Here, sit down!"

From his and Deborah's reaction Tansy could not gauge their mood, they appeared to be as wary of her as she was of them. She started speaking, rapidly, frightened that if she did not say what she planned, immediately, she may not find the courage.

"I've come to say sorry." She scanned their faces but still she could not read them. "I only thought of my career and, that it was a good story," she quoted, mocking herself. "What I did was inconsiderate and miscalculated." She broke off, hearing Reuben's accusations, accusations that she had played over and over, once again. She felt tears welling and, embarrassed, resisted wiping them away. Jacob was speaking but she found it difficult to concentrate.

"Perhaps it was, but it's in the past. We've long forgotten that episode," she heard Jacob saying.

"It was brave of you to come here," Deborah added.

Tansy took a deep breath. It steadied her. Then, each word drawn independently from her she said. "I haven't really been able to write. I had to come." She addressed Jacob, "Craig says that you understand. What is it that you understand?"

"A young person's ambition. Yours is not an easy profession when it comes to distinguishing newsworthy stories from infringement on personal privacy."

Jacob no longer felt like a figure in the distance. Some of Tansy's confidence returned. "I've learnt that lesson," she admitted.

"Don't be too hard on yourself." Tansy heard the warmth return to Deborah's voice. "The ideas that you absorbed from Jacob, they've gone a long way." Deborah smiled, but Tansy felt at a loss.

"What do you mean?" She looked from Deborah to Jacob.

Deborah had sounded amused rather than condemnatory. "The upheaval in the art world. It's not only here that local artists are being supported. The momentum that started in the Isle of Man is spreading and who knows its limits. You can take some credit for that. Didn't Reuben tell you?"

At the sound of his name Tansy felt choked. "I thought Reuben said that he was going to Dubai."

Deborah must have picked up from her strained voice that Tansy was struggling. "Oh, my dear!" Tansy heard her say. "Did you and Reuben…?" She stopped and turned to Jacob. "That explains everything. Reuben broke off with Tansy and that's why he left so suddenly. What we thought was just an idea, he put into action almost immediately. It did not make sense at the time."

Tansy was not sure that this was news that she wanted to hear. Jacob continued, however.

"He knows the full story now. Abigail has seen him during her travels. If anything I am to blame for inflicting my lifelong theories on a susceptible and receptive mind."

"You mean me?" Tansy asked him, bewildered. Then after a pause she said, "It won't make any difference to Reuben. He was adamant. And he was right." She saw that both Jacob and Deborah were looking at her expectantly. "But what really matters to me is your opinion. And now I must go."

Deborah halted her. "I think the girls would like to see you. They were very fond of you."

Tansy was not sure that she could face yet more accusatory confrontations but she could not refuse Deborah. It was part of her penance.

Tansy stood inside the door of the sitting room where Matty and Florrie were sitting. They stared at her nervously. "Everything's all right now," she told them.

Matty was the first to move. She was more restrained than she had been in the summer but she came close to

Tansy and looked up at her. "I am so happy. We missed you."

Florrie joined her, tall and composed, and smiled although still guarded. "I really want to get away from here and find a job in Glasgow. I don't suppose the room in your flat is still free?"

TWENTY-SIX

Glasgow was, even two days after Hogmanay, suffering from inertia. Few buses were running, taxis were scarce and, as Tansy travelled from the airport into the city, even the sight of people on the streets was a rarity. The city, grey, wet and dreary, seemed to have closed down never to recover again the vibrancy that emanated from it during the days leading up to New Year. If she had not some interviews to conduct and a deadline to meet, Tansy would have delayed her return. It had been a late decision, to join her parents for Christmas, and the available flights had contributed to her arriving on one of the most depressing days in the year's calendar.

At the airport, Tansy waited in a queue for the bus until she feared she would succumb to frostbite. Eventually she crossed to the taxi rank and, approaching the other passengers, found someone who was prepared to share a lift. By the time she reached her flat it had been dark for hours. She had forgotten, while in the sunshine, that daylight disappeared in the afternoon. None of this helped her spirits, and when she picked up her mail and recognised Reuben's writing, all the turmoil of emotions with which she had struggled, resurfaced.

There was nothing in the cupboards except for a bottle of wine. She switched on every heater and her electric blanket and huddled under a rug on the sofa. She separated the bills and circulars and put them to one side, and placed Reuben's letter with another handwritten envelope whose writing she did not recognise, within reach. She sat wondering why she had left the warmth and companionship of her family.

She picked up Reuben's letter and held it. Why would he be writing after all these months? She feared that perhaps something else had occurred to him for which he was going to blame her. She could hardly bear any more. Yet she had been reassured by Jacob and Deborah that she was no longer considered the criminal figure that she had been depicted by Reuben.

Slowly she lifted the edges of the envelope and took out the letter. Quickly she skimmed it, the writing covered both sides and it ended 'with love'. She stopped shivering. She read the letter again more carefully. Reuben had spent Christmas with his parents and had been shown her articles, particularly the one in which Tansy had vindicated her actions. He told her that his parents were no longer angry. His antagonism, he said, had been on their behalf. Time and his instincts enabled him to see the affair in perspective and, combined with his parents' acceptance of events, helped his decision to ask her to forgive him.

Tansy sat and looked into the meagre red glow of the two-bar electric heater. It was difficult to reconcile this letter with the months of misery that she had endured. She had experienced the anguish of guilt and had lost much of her sense of self-worth. However, deep within her, she felt that their relationship could heal and the heavy load that she had carried on her shoulders lightened.

Eventually she picked up the second envelope. It had been forwarded from the office. The writing was neat and she had been addressed formally as 'Miss'. She opened the envelope and took out a white card with an invitation in embossed printing. Slowly she read, 'Phillip Glentenmont invites Miss Tansy Witt to the inaugural exhibition of paintings at Manquill Castle.' There followed the date and time and RSVP. Tansy placed it on the arm of the chair. She reached into the envelope of Reuben's letter and unfolded an air ticket for Dubai. Wriggling free of the rug which was wrapped around her shoulders Tansy held the ticket in one hand and the invitation in the other, and switched her attention from one to the other, pondering on Reuben's change of heart and remembering her single encounter on the Isle of Man.

She saw a message on the reverse side of the invitation and as she read it she smiled.

'Tansy! Do come, Phillip.'

Acknowledgements

I would like to thank Lois Aitkenhead and Sarah Crothers, for their enthusiasm after reading the early draft of this novel, Becky Tabram, for her careful help and encouragement, and Jenny Haviland for her scrutiny of the manuscript.

Also to acknowledge the companionship of all the members of the Glenkens writing group over six years under our inspiring tutor, and now friend, Margaret Elphinstone.

The front cover image was painted by the artist Henry Israel.

I would like to thank editor Sam Carter; although I have been unable to meet him in person, the courtesy of his emails and his respectful manner gained my trust.